COMMON SENSE

THE KEY TO SAVING OUR REPUBLIC

DAVID P. MCMULLAN

authorHOUSE®

AuthorHouse™
1663 Liberty Drive
Bloomington, IN 47403
www.authorhouse.com
Phone: 833-262-8899

© 2022 David P. McMullan. All rights reserved.

No part of this book may be reproduced, stored in a retrieval system, or transmitted by any means without the written permission of the author.

Published by AuthorHouse 07/05/2022

ISBN: 978-1-6655-6410-6 (sc)
ISBN: 978-1-6655-6411-3 (e)

Print information available on the last page.

Any people depicted in stock imagery provided by Getty Images are models, and such images are being used for illustrative purposes only.
Certain stock imagery © Getty Images.

This book is printed on acid-free paper.

Because of the dynamic nature of the Internet, any web addresses or links contained in this book may have changed since publication and may no longer be valid. The views expressed in this work are solely those of the author and do not necessarily reflect the views of the publisher, and the publisher hereby disclaims any responsibility for them.

CONTENTS

FOREWORD

We are presently in a war with a philosophical enemy that has taken hold of one of our stalwart political parties.

This is not a **Republican** or **Democratic** issue that offers differences of opinion over how our **Republic** should prosper going forward. It's more serious than that.

Our success is based on a vibrant two party system in **America** that provides both a difference of opinion on key issues and also serves as a safeguard from any one party having too much power or losing their way.

The one thing we could always count on was that members of both parties love our system of government and love our country above all else.

The rise of the **Progressive Movement**, which has taken hold under the **Democratic** banner, is one that not only finds both our country and its system of government lacking but is attempting to transform America from a **Capitalistic** nation, that has prospered for centuries, into a nation that is more dependent on government and less freedom oriented.

In order to prevent the reimagining of **America**, we first must bring the **Progressive Movement** into the light and expose their beliefs for all to see. This is not the **Democratic Party** of John F. Kennedy or even Bill Clinton, for that matter.

We can no longer remain the silent majority. We need to raise our voices for all to hear and stop the changing of **America**, once and for all, before this movement succeeds in altering our **DNA** from a nation founded on individual rights and freedoms into a nation of handouts and entitlements, depending on others to get by.

When you remove our desire to succeed, you end up with a nation that no longer has the will to excel.

America is a **Meritocracy**, which is a good thing, and we need to preserve **America** as a land of promise and opportunity for all.

David P. McMullan

CHAPTER ONE

Introduction

We have survived and prospered for more than two centuries now under a system of government that not only permitted different points of view but fostered their inclusion in determining our decisions.

At present, we have a two party system that serves as a viable means of preventing any particular party from going off the rails and changing the course of **American** politics.

While our **Democratic** and **Republican** parties approach running the country from different perspectives, I have never doubted everyone's love of country and belief that our system of government was the correct path for us to take, deserving our protection at all costs.

Over the past few decades, there has been a movement away from the middle and toward more extreme views of **America**, our **Republic** and the validity that our system of government is worth preserving.

This change in philosophy is dangerous, in my opinion, because it questions the basic principles that has made **America** the most prosperous and powerful nation on the planet.

One particular movement is gaining momentum and comes from the far left wing of our **Democratic Party**. It threatens our present way of life with a message and philosophy that could alter the delicate balance that has always existed between the **Democratic** and **Republican** parties.

Our country works best when we govern from the middle, a place where most **Americans** presently reside. If power were to shift to either extreme, we run the risk of destroying who we are as a nation and removing our position of strength on the world stage, something no country will benefit from since **America** offers the world innovative and creative advantages as well as powerful support for those in need.

The danger we face today, in my opinion, is the rise of **Progressivism** and its apparent takeover of the **Democratic Party**.

We live in a politically charged time where just about everything has a political connection.

While this cultural change has been progressing for decades, the recent rise to power of the **Progressives** has placed their entire movement on steroids and left the rest of us, for the first time, with a view of just how damaging this can be to our country, our freedom and the future of our **Republic**.

It is no longer okay to remain on the sidelines and observe**.**

In the past, where we could ponder the absurdity of the **Socialist and Marxist** philosophies without fear of them becoming law, it was okay to point out those absurdities and dismiss them without a second thought.

Today, it appears that their movement has made significant inroads into the **Democratic Party** beyond anything we thought possible.

Now, with control of the **White House** and both branches of the Legislature under **Democratic** rule, we are learning just how much influence the **Progressives** have behind the scenes of power in Washington.

There are numerous danger signs being flashed before our eyes that are being hidden behind a cloak of deception that needs to be uncovered for all to see.

This book hopes to expose the **Progressives** for who they are and bring all of their attempts at changing **America** into focus.

I still believe that **America** will never accept **Socialism** as a way of life if the average **American** could see it for what it is rather than what it's pretending to be.

We can no longer afford to look at **Progressivism** as a harmless movement lacking teeth. They have serious advocates in positions of power and their teeth are sharp and ready to bit

Common Sense

There is a master plan by the **Progressives** that is being carried out, behind the scenes, that we must find a way to expose to the masses.

While it would be great if we had a **Media** that valued truth over political preferences, unfortunately, that ship has sailed and there is no longer a clear view of its mast on the horizon.

It is my belief that the answer, along with a well armed and motivated vocal majority, lies in our most treasured gift from **GOD** that separates us from the rest of the creatures that share our planet - **COMMON SENSE**.

It is my belief that **COMMON SENSE** is non political and a part of our nature that cannot be ignored or pushed aside for expediency purposes. In laymen's terms it is our **GUT** talking or what some might call our instinctual tendencies.

MAN is the only life form on the planet that possesses this gift. Every other species of life has an advanced form of instinct that is there to protect them from the dangers that surround them, which has them fighting a daily battle for survival.

Man might face less life and death situations on a daily basis but the need to identify threats remain.

Because of that, nature has not permitted our natural instincts to evolve at the same rate but we have the added benefit of **COMMON SENSE** that allows us to evaluate instinctual reactions rather than just experiencing them.

When we are faced with these internal feelings that warn us that things are not what they appear to be, we have our **COMMON SENSE** gene that, if allowed to express itself, can help us to understand what is really going on and help us to better respond to these feelings.

While the animals have distractions that interfere with their instincts, such as the need for water, **MAN** is not without its distractions.

Our primary distraction is our **Intellect**. We can talk ourselves out of what our **GUT** tells us to be the truth, thus ignoring our **COMMON SENSE** gene in favor of our desire to believe otherwise.

The use of intellectual rhetoric as a tool to control the masses has been in place for decades. Politicians have been using it for years on both sides of the aisle, trying to convince us that their opinions and proposed political ideology is the right path for us to follow.

Sometimes they push too hard and we can see the real message behind the curtain.

At times they succeed in convincing us that our intellect is mightier than our **COMMON SENSE** gene and we are better off ignoring it in favor of their rhetoric.

Its time for us to abandon the label of silent majority and become proactive by reminding all **Americans** that words, no matter how well they are delivered or how well they may mask the truth, are just words that might be hiding the real message that's left unsaid.

The **COMMON SENSE** moments that will be pointed out along the way are there to remove the veil that is in front of all of the falsehoods, exaggerations, and emotional pleas, attempting to hide the facts from view.

It will take **ALL** of us **Patriots** to speak up and offer everyone a more rational approach, if we plan on exposing the **Progressives** for the frauds they are.

I truly believe that the average liberal and moderate **Democrat** has no desire to allow our country to take a turn toward **Socialism**.

The **Progressives** are aware of this, thus the need to hide their true purpose, in order to keep their moderate party members from abandoning ship.

Hopefully, exposing the truth from a **COMMON SENSE** point of view will be sufficient to change the minds of the less **Progressive** liberals and independents among us who have the power to swing the needle back to the middle, a safer place where most **Americans** reside anyway.

With any luck, we can preserve our **Republic** from being destroyed on our watch.

THE MEDIA

Many of these **Progressive** ideas should be obvious to the masses and, under normal conditions result in outrage, if not for the **Media**.

Everyday **Americans** are educated enough to put the brakes on these outlandish proposals if not for the deceptive **Media** that has chosen to drop their mask of neutrality in favor of partisanship on a huge scale.

I, for one, believe that a neutral press alone would keep the **Progressives** at bay.

When the partisan spin of the politicians are amplified by a partisan press, the message not only gets repeated but validated, as well. It serves the purpose similar to having a second opinion under the guise of journalistic neutrality.

Saving the **Republic** is going to have to fall on the shoulders of patriotic **Americans** that make up the **SILENT MAJORITY**.

Waiting for others to take up the mantle of truth will leave all of us with a reimagined system of government that will be unrecognizable and difficult to dismantle.

How Do We Begin?

It begins with understanding what the **Progressive** agenda is and how they plan on using it.

They hope to turn this country from a **Free Republic** into a government controlled **Marxist** regime by dissolving most of our freedoms before we are aware of the change, replacing those freedoms with government programs that limit our potential and make us more dependent on those in power.

Do not be fooled by their use of **Socialism** as an acceptable end to their journey.

While **Socialism** is basically economic by nature, their end game, which is **Marxism,** transforms everything we take for granted in **America**, including our freedoms, into a power based control center that forces compliance over individual choices.

When your goal is government control over everything of importance, you are heading farther down the tracks, passing the **Socialism Stop** entirely, so that the train can make it all the way to **Marxism**. They have no intention of stopping or looking back once they see any progress along the way.

The old adage, **Ignorance is Bliss**, might be fine for the little things but disastrous when we are dealing with the future of our nation.

The **Progressive** movement begins with a belief that our **Republic**, which is bolstered by **Capitalism**, relies too much on the freedoms of the individual and less on the controls being implemented by the government. In other words, its time to do away with the **Republic** and its capital driven support system.

You cannot successfully institute **Socialism**, or its more restrictive cousin **Marxism**, as long as the people remain in control of their own destinies.

How best to create an atmosphere that will allow the P**rogressives** the ammunition they need to convince the masses that the government is better at providing them with services than they are?

When your goal is to control everything of importance, deception is the only answer. **Americans** will never give up their freedoms unless they can be fooled into believing that there is no possible option left to them except compliance.

In order to accomplish such a cosmic shift, the **Progressives** need to break down barriers to freedom such as our faith and our sense of belonging and self worth.

Though complicated and difficult to obtain, they have been working on accomplishing these objectives for decades.

Things are different today as they finally are in charge of the big stuff.

They can proceed at warp speed for the first time and, if luck is on their side, they might change the landscape before anyone realizes that this is no longer the **America** they once knew.

There are a number of barriers that stand in their way. These barriers need to become less significant in our lives if the **Progressives** are to change **America**.

This is not a simple task as these three barriers, which I call the three **C'S**, are second nature to most of us and will not be marginalized easily.

They are:

- **Capitalism**
- **Christianity**
- **Control (the loss of individual freedoms)**

Trying to change millions of **Americans**, who have lived free and who are blessed with personal freedom, into believing that many of their freedoms are better left to the government, requires a massive campaign that will slowly begin to pit one **American** against another as we lose sight of what it is that makes us such a great country.

An Example of Progressives saying one thing and meaning another

A perfect example is the **Progressive** campaign to re-imagine the election process.

On the surface, their plan of shifting from a state controlled process to a federally centralized process, can appear rational if you can somehow convince the masses that our present system is flawed on a number of levels, especially when it comes to being fair and equal to everyone.

They have been working on this for decades already by slowly modifying **ELECTION DAY** from a single day event into a number of days that allow more people to vote without the need to show up on that one Tuesday in November.

Most States now offer early voting that can span out for a number of weeks prior to Election Day.

While this has created the desired result of removing that all important day from the equation as being critical to the process, it falls short with the **Progressive Agenda** of controlling the process in such a way as to permit them to influence the outcome when necessary.

While it is true that you have more days to vote, you still have to follow all of the rules by showing up at the polling place, identifying yourself as an **American** citizen with a proper ID and finally signing in. All of this before being able to cast your vote for the candidate of your choice.

Remember, the **Progressives** have been playing the long game for decades.

Spreading out the voting opportunities has proven to be so successful to this point that I doubt anyone would be happy if their state decided to abandon this newly earned perk and require everyone back to the polls on that one Tuesday in November.

The next step in their plan was to expand a minor part of the election process into something a lot more impactful.

We already had a limited number of mail-in ballots coming from citizens who were not going to be in state on Election Day. While many of these mail-in ballots come from military personnel and those working or traveling away from their home state, the ability to cast your vote via mail is a necessity for those that are away and still looking to exercise their right as a citizen.

For a voter to do so, this is not an easy process. They have to request a ballot be sent to them and they have to provide the necessary documentation required,

including proof of identity and a valid reason for the request.

Voting for our elected officials is one of the more important duties required of our citizens. The process requires an effort on our part and should not be so simple as to replace one's thoughtful and intentional desire to be part of the elective process.

This is the reason that elections only manage to capture a portion of the electorate. Those not interested in the process or the candidates should not partake in the process just because they have a right to do so.

They need to make that concerted effort because to do anything less would diminish the importance of the process and open the door to the possibility of fraud and deception, neither of which deserves a place in our electoral system.

While national elections capture a greater percentage of voters than local elections, the numbers are never much higher than the 60-70% of the eligible voters.

Sometimes in the off years when the ballots only have local races with limited impact, the numbers can be as low as 20-30% of the voters turning out.

The **Progressives** saw this mail-in option as a potential home run for them going forward if they could create a reason to have it expanded.

There are many potential voters out there that are either too lazy or not sufficiently motivated to leave their house to vote for anyone. Being able to stay at home and mail in their vote seemed like a better chance of expanding the number of ballots received for any election.

It is my opinion that many of the newly **Progressive** voters are younger, less patriotic, less religious and more prone to apathy. If left to their own resources, they may not be motivated enough to vote because of the complications required for verification.

How these younger voters became so P**rogressive** lies in an ongoing indoctrination process in our schools over the past few decades that will be addressed later on and in more detail.

The lack of discipline and motivation among younger voters has played out over the years. Recently, we have noticed their lack of discipline when Bernie Sanders, the most recognized **Socialist** in the country, sprung into prominence.

We all know how Sanders influenced young minds with his push to rally them to his beliefs in the colleges and universities. The indoctrination that is going on in our educational institutions has been thorough and far reaching.

When push came to shove, these radical supporters for Bernie never seem to make it to the voting booth in large enough numbers as to sway the election in their favor, even in some of the primaries.

Can you imagine how successful the **Progressives** could be if they were permitted to allow all of these young students to cast their vote from the comfort of their dorm room without having to lift a finger?

The first step requires turning mail-in voting into an acceptable option. Thanks to the recent pandemic, I would say **Mission Accomplished.** This past election of 2020 saw a record number of mail-in ballots cast across the country.

The second and more difficult task requires softening the voting requirements that are too restrictive for their needs, especially the need for every voter to have to request a ballot, verify their identity and provide an acceptable reason for requiring the mail-in ballot.

The **Progressive's** initial attempt, which began prior to the pandemic, was one that stretched the credibility meter a bit too far, in my opinion.

They saw, as a primary obstacle, the verification process that requires only registered voters with a proper photo ID being permitted to cast a vote.

Not only did the **Progressives** have to motivate their younger supporters to request and fill out their mail-in ballots, they had to get them to register properly with the state before anything meaningful could happen.

If verification could be watered down or even eliminated, then they could bring most of their campus supporters along for the ride and up their chances of getting their people elected.

Failing to find a more viable option to convince the masses of the need to soften the requirements, the **Progressives** chose to turn their attention back to one of their tried and true fall back positions of blaming anything that blocks their agenda on **Racism.**

When their acolytes began complaining how the need for a photo ID was prejudicial to a large number of minorities who were unable to meet such a requirement, the time to call them out for such a ridiculous claim was stalled by their partners in deception, the main stream **Media.**

While many **Republicans** and **Conservatives** were quite vocal, the vast majority of the population that either are less interested in the political landscape or choose to get their news from headlines or sound bites, were being told a different story, one that is so ludicrous as to suggest that such an argument actually has merit.

We have come to our first **COMMON SENSE** moment that needs to be passed along to our moderate and independent friends without any political edge to the discussion. The only thing political is for them to remember who is putting forth this nonsense and why. Can you ever trust anyone that believes this to be true?

COMMON SENSE MOMENT

When someone pretends that there is a significant number of American citizens out there that are interested in exercising their right to vote and are functioning in our society without any form of identification, they need to be reminded that no such person exist that is not presently living under a bridge somewhere, homeless and without any means of supporting themselves.

While I dare say that, in my opinion, many of our homeless do have identification of some sort and not without any valid means of identifying themselves, I doubt that the small number of people with no ID have placed the need to vote in our elections at the top of their list of issues.

Do not forget that the Progressives complaining about this slight on our less fortunate citizens have also insinuated that the less

prepared among us are primarily minorities and that allows them to claim that the photo ID requirement is another form of racism.

Now here's the truth that anyone with a COMMON SENSE gene in their body cannot properly ignore:

- *You cannot function in our society without proper identification.*
- *Every time you visit a hospital or a doctor for an illness, need to get medicine to help you, have to enter a facility of any sort that is government run or, in most cases, privately run like a bank, you need to prove who you are.*
- *If you ever want to rent, buy or obtain just about anything, you need to tell someone who you are and prove it.*

How can their be a significant number of citizens living their life this way that would warrant the need to completely disrupt our electoral process in order to accommodate them?

If our COMMON SENSE gene tells us that this makes no sense then what is the REAL reason they are attempting to make us change the voter ID requirement?

It's not to allow thousands of underserved Americans the right to vote but it is obvious that they do not want the rest of us to know the real reason for this charade.

What their deception can assure all of us is the reason left unsaid would not be acceptable to most Americans or they would just tells us what it is and avoid the ruse completely.

Try to explain to every American how a loose and non-regulated election, where its possible for a number of ballots to be received that might not be properly executed by one of our citizens, is good for the country? Such an argument, if our people understood its implications, would fall on deaf ears.

Why are the Progressives using Race to sell their false claim? Telling them that the process is racist does not require the need to provide the details. The accusation is enough to sway the socially conscious and factually deficient masses. Just shut up and obey. No one wants to be called a Racist.

The real reason, in my opinion, is the need for the Progressives to control the election process if they are to succeed in securing the necessary power they so covet.

If they could count on their message to be well received and motivational enough to garner the support they require, there would be no reason to muddy the waters and create a system that can only be described as insufficient and less secure than the one we have chosen to use for the past few centuries.

You have to ask that all important question of WHY, if not to allow the opportunity for fraud and deception to permeate the election process?

It's definitely not the need to find a way for the dozen or more citizens in this country of 330 million, with no form of identification, the right to vote.

The only answer I can come up with for a loose and less regulated election system lies in the possibility that such lax requirements for proper verification might lead to potential fraud.

I'm open to another possibility if anyone has a better reason for such a strategy. It can't be the belief that we are leaving a dozen or more citizens behind.

We need to hammer home this point to anyone who would listen. There is no reason to bring politics into the conversation.

If you cannot find a viable answer that makes any sense for disrupting our entire election process, the next question to ask is WHY do it at all?

Rational Americans who see no logical reason for change can fill in the rest by themselves. I doubt they will come up with a better reason.

Americans have always understood that we are not perfect.

Having said that, we have always believed that our way of life and our system of government has led to centuries of success, growth and freedom few nations, if any, can claim as their own. Who we are and what we stand for are the primary reasons millions of people would rather live here than anywhere else.

Faced with such a daunting task, the **Progressives** need to slowly break down our preconceived notions of **America** and leave the masses open to the possibility that the basic principles that have been the foundation of our country for centuries, could do with some tweaking.

Once you accept that notion, the necessary propaganda campaign can begin in earnest and the wheels can be put in motion to systematically change our nation from a **Republic** into a **Socialist-Marxist** regime that will lead us, in my opinion, to ruin.

There are two requirements necessary for the **Progressives** to obtain their goal of convincing **Americans** that the Federal Government, not only knows best, but is the only option that can restore order and stability to a fractured nation:

- **Fear**
- **Division**

In the upcoming chapters I will attempt to expose all of their plans and provide everyone with non-political **COMMON SENSE** moments that can be used to bring their ultimate goal into the light of day.

When you argue your points from a political perspective, those not in line with your beliefs tend to shut you down as offering just another talking point for your political point of view.

When you argue based on **COMMON SENSE**, there is less objection and less chance that they can dismiss your ideas out of hand. Let's take them down with the truth, not political bias.

CHAPTER TWO

When the goal of the **Progressive Movemen**t is the transformation of the country we all thought we knew, you cannot just put it all out there and hope for universal support.

Having a position of power in our present **Administration** offers them the bully pulpit that allows their voice to be heard but does not guarantee that their voice will be accepted or embraced.

If they plan on removing most of our freedoms through attrition, they need to disguise their motives carefully or the outrage could stop them in their tracks.

Americans would not take kindly to anyone challenging their **God** given individual freedoms that were promised by our **Founding Fathers**.

Government Control

Our **Founding Fathers** understood just how dangerous it would be for government to grow out of control and create a country where the people were subservient to those in charge.

Limited government was always their plan. The **Federal Government** needed to be in place for the **BIG** things such as defense of the nation and protection of our liberties.

State's Rights in a **Republic** are paramount to us succeeding. The framers knew how important this was as our country grew into what we know as **America** today and what Ronald Reagan once referred to as "**The Shining City on the Hill**".

Once you get beyond the really big things, the people need their local government to manage their regional needs including police protection, education and elections, to name a few.

The **Progressive's** plan is to grow government beyond what the **Founding Fathers** had planned. The more the government controls, the less freedom the people have to influence their own direction and agenda.

There are two ideologies that form the foundation of the **Progressive Movement**:

- **Socialism**
- **Marxism**

Both of these ideologies are cut from the same cloth, each one getting more restrictive and more authoritarian as they make their way toward total control.

The less restrictive is **Socialism,** though still nothing short of a major change to our system of government. This has always been a dirty word that **Americans** considered inconceivable just a few years ago.

The thought of giving up any of our individual freedoms to the government seemed like a pipe dream that only a handful of the more extreme among us thought was a good idea.

In fact, when **Bernie Sanders** appeared on the scene as the voice of the young and inexperienced among us, he preached the values of **Socialism** from an uneducated and unrealistic vantage point, failing to list the shortfalls that anyone who has ever lived under a **Socialist** regime knew from first hand experience.

Free healthcare and free education sounds like a great idea as long as you ignore the fact that none of this comes without a price or a loss of personal freedom.

Our student population, always looking for a more radical movement to get behind, especially if that movement opposes the status quo, took hold of his message and began to use it as the mantra for change.

As for the adults in the room, in particular those that have immigrated here from suppressive countries that practiced their own form of **Socialism**, Bernie's philosophy fell on deaf ears.

I smile to this day when Bernie calls himself a **Democratic Socialist.** Using those two words together in order to validate his version of **Socialism** is just another attempt at deception.

They are so diametrically opposed to one another that attempting to convince anyone that they could exist in harmony requires an ignorance of world history, seeing how **Socialism** has never succeeded anywhere in the world.

Socialism requires the **"all knowing "** government to provide for the masses from cradle to grave by maximizing the government's power base to control all of the important aspects of life, including education, healthcare, national security, welfare, childcare and any other service that provides assistance where we once relied on our work ethic and ingenuity to succeed.

When you remove freedom of choice, replacing it with equitable outcomes that inhibit ones initiative and desire to excel, you create a nation that leaves all of the power in the hands of bureaucrats that no longer need your approval to operate.

Placing all of that power in the hands of a few is the exact opposite of what our **Founding Fathers** intended for **America**.

Common Sense Moment

Has our Federal Government, when overstepping their original purpose, ever run anything successfully, much less profitably? (The Post Office and Amtrak come to mind)

The problem with bureaucrats being in charge of anything leaves a lot to be desired, especially if it requires fiscal control and a level of expertise that carries with it responsibility and accountability.

When you are never forced to maintain a P & L statement, never have to operate within your means or never have to worry as to where the money will come from when you decide on a course of action and the feasibility of that course, you always get into trouble.

Remember where the government gets the funds they need to operate. It comes from you and I and if they squander or mismanage things, they just collect more from us or print the money necessary to make up the shortfall, either one of these scenarios is terrible for the economic health of the country.

Giving them more to be responsible for does not seem like a good idea under any circumstances.

Margaret Thatcher once said that **Socialism** works well until the government begins to run out of other peoples money.

A cradle to grave system of government is extremely expensive and requires funding that ultimately grows beyond the ability to generate enough taxes to cover the outlay.

That brings us to the **Progressive** war on **Capitalism**.

Capitalism

In order for the **Progressives** to succeed, they need to find a way to minimize and ultimately eliminate our **Capitalistic** economy that depends on individual effort and creativity in the marketplace.

Capitalism depends on our individual freedoms to choose and to control our own destiny even if those choices turn out to be lacking.

As individuals in a free society, we choose how much education we deem is suitable for our needs and decide on what careers to pursue, if any.

Capitalism allows us to change our direction multiple times, if necessary, and to begin again if need be.

For example, how hard we work and how essential we can make ourselves to our employer goes a long way in determining our success or failure over our lifetime.

Anyone that achieves success beyond their expectations have been able to make themselves invaluable to their companies and that gets them noticed for their efforts and rewarded for their importance to the corporate objective.

The **Progressive** idea that everyone deserves the same opportunities, no matter the path they have chosen to take, is ridiculous.

The opportunity to succeed is there for everyone but requires action on their part to choose a path commensurate with those opportunities.

Opportunity does not become a choice opened to everyone who failed to prepare for the challenges. Students who study Philosophy cannot decide on a career in Engineering and expect to have viable options without the necessary pre-requisites.

Can someone who wants to be a Doctor expect to get into medical school having no prior training or having chose a different educational path that did not leave them properly prepared for the task and workload that was to come?

In a **Capitalist** society, many companies offer growth opportunities that are open to everyone within their company if they choose to do the work and to prove to management that they have what it takes to do the job.

There are thousands of success stories of employees who have started at the bottom and managed to reach the boardroom based on their work ethic, drive and learned skills on the job that propelled them to the top.

Success requires a balance of good management and capable, motivated employees that have the right skill and work ethic to propel the company forward. There's no such thing as a mediocre work ethic creating financial success for the shareholders.

Remember the goal of the **Progressives**. A free society that fosters individual freedom of choice is not an ideal partner for achieving success. That's why they love the **UNIONS.**

Under the Union philosophy, **Longevity** (**Tenure** when discussing education) rules over work ethic, creating an atmosphere where mediocrity becomes the order of the day.

Under the **Union** banner, workers who excel at their job can find themselves without a supportive partner, especially if their success reflects unfavorably on their fellow workers.

The over achiever tends to create animosity among their fellow **union** members who see no reason to over-perform when it serves no purpose or provides no added compensation other than personal pride and achievement.

You rarely find a **union** that rewards better workers with more pay and benefits than their fellow brethren.

I'm sure, if given the permission from the **union**, the company that is reaping the increased productivity would gladly reward the over achiever for their efforts, to the detriment of their less productive **union** members.

None of these principles, which should be the goal of every worker and company, are fostered or nurtured under the **UNION** blanket. Over-achieving **union** members will not earn greater pay and more opportunities. In fact, they may actually achieve themselves right out the door.

If a **union** worker earns more money than another, it's usually based on longevity, not performance. That can only foster mediocrity, something that blends well with the **Socialist** concept of equitable outcomes for everyone.

A Battle between the HAVES and the HAVE NOTS

America is considered around the world to be the land of opportunity. That requires a level of freedom that permits every citizen a chance to succeed and to prosper depending on their work ethic and educational prowess.

While we are not perfect and should recognize that everyone has not been afforded all of the necessary opportunities our constitution demands over the past few centuries, we are far from an oppressive and authoritarian country than many of those in the **Progressive** movement would like you to believe.

The **Progressives** have been working on the neutralization of **Capitalism** for decades.

How many years is it now that they have been spewing the idea that the rich need to pay their fair share. When questioned about what that actually means, you never get a satisfactory answer.

How much should the rich pay in taxes? How much should they be allowed to keep?

On the surface this appears to be a straight forward attempt to collect more taxes from the fortunate among us.

If you listen carefully to the tone used by the **Progressives** when discussing **Corporate America**, you can hear the disdain they have for just about every aspect of our **Capitalistic** Society.

These wealthy individuals who run our companies and live their lives of luxury think they are better than the rest of us and represent **America's** version of Royalty overseeing their peasant class, which constitutes everyone else.

They would like all of us to believe that it's the wealthy corporate managers who take advantage of their workers whenever possible, forcing them to work for sub-standard wages, requiring them to generate the profits that keep the companies running but never permitting the workers to share in the bounty.

Has anyone ever studied the **Communist Manifesto**?

When the **Communist** movement, which is the more severe and restrictive extension of **Socialism,** tried desperately to infiltrate **Europe** at the beginning of the Twentieth Century, with their philosophy of communal sharing over individual accomplishments, they chose to attack manufacturing and their unfair treatment of the less fortunate laborer, hoping to create a revolt among the workers against the establishment.

As the years go by with the constant slings and arrows being thrown their way, the public is beginning to accept the possibility that **Corporate America** might actually be ruthless and manipulative, offering nothing of value to those not successful or wealthy enough to earn a place in their universe.

We used to look up to those that achieved greatness and success as people we emulate, not loathe.

We all wanted to be them and most of **America** realized that their jobs were due to someone who achieved greatness and needed them to keep the machines running and the coffers full.

The **Progressives** have been playing the long game for decades and the fruits of their labor are beginning to pay dividends. We are gradually developing a wedge between the classes and that is the first step to pitting the worker against the establishment and ensuring that the **bond** between them remains tenuous at best.

The birth of the WOKE phenomenon and its ugly stepchild Cancel Culture

The **Progressives** have been gradually losing their patience with the long game when it comes to **Capitalism**.

While the division they seek is slowly taking hold, they are looking to find a way of speeding up the process without showing their hand.

They found just the right tool by creating the **WOKE** movement as a false snapshot into the heart and soul of **America** and supporting it with the most divisive enforcement scam ever to hit the shores of our great land, that of **Cancel Culture**.

Common Sense Moment

I don't want everyone to get the idea that the Progressive assault on Corporate America is not without its supporters.

There are numerous companies that operate internationally who are more concerned with the global marketplace rather than the American marketplace.

When their loyalty lies elsewhere, the outrage over the possible

transformation of America takes a backseat to their own global mission statement, which may place their priorities elsewhere.

In my opinion, they are playing a dangerous game. While the Progressive assault on Corporate America might be aimed elsewhere for the time being, their desire to minimize the freedoms of all companies will lead them eventually to the doors of EVERY company, friend or foe.

In the end, if the Progressive succeed in changing America, they will not be spared because they played along for now.

The world economy will not be in a better place if America falls off its perch of dominance in the marketplace.

Any view that ignores that fact is a view that, in my opinion, is short sighted and lacks vision.

Its important for you to understand that the true **Progressive** followers believe in their movement and have totally bought into their agenda. They have been forced fed one opinion only and they have bought it hook, line and sinker.

Because of their fervent beliefs, the **Progressives** view just about anyone that does not believe in their ideals or chosen direction for the country to be not just wrong, but evil and dangerous.

While that includes **ALL** of the country that leans to the right, it also includes many of the more moderates in their party that might consider themselves to be centrist by nature.

When you are fighting evil, there are little rules that apply to your behavior that one might consider to be unacceptable. In other words, no attack is off the table when your goal is to crush evil at all cost.

The **WOKE** movement, which is supported by **Big Tech** and communicated through **Social Media** by thousands of trolls who are more than willing to point out their less than **WOKE** fellow citizens, has succeeded in getting their message across to the masses while fostering division among us, a critical tool for the **Progressives** to succeed.

Their primary objective, in my opinion, is to breakdown many of the norms and past beliefs about both our country and our citizens which threatens their ultimate goal of reimagining our form of government.

If they are to have us move away from a **Republic** that is supported by **Capitalism**, toward a more **Socialistic** view of cradle to grave dependency that requires submission and less individual freedoms, they need us to reject past norms and values for greener pastures, or so they claim.

Here's where things get more complicated and problematic. Just identifying these **anti-woke i**ssues that go against their ideals are not sufficient. They require consequences, another word for punishment, for those that refuse to bend to their wishes and accept their warped ideology as fact.

That's where **Cancel Culture** comes in. Now they have a weapon that can beat their non-believers into submission and force them to acquiesce to their demands.

What the **Progressives** needed from the **WOKE** movement, along with the newly created **Cancel Culture** weapon to accomplish, was the systematic breakdown of our beliefs and values that were in the way of their ultimate plan to reimagine **America**.

These values and beliefs include:

- **Family**
- **Respect for others**
- **Language that unites rather than divides**
- **Patriotism**
- **Religion**
- **Individual responsibility and personal work ethic**

The **WOKE** agenda is designed to accomplish their objective through:

- **Secularism**
- **Collective verses the Family**
- **Division among the masses**
- **Racism**
- **Rewriting of history**
- **A culture of dependency replacing personal responsibility**

The **Progressive's** need to grow the government to a massive size that will guarantee that this newly formed **Oligarchy**, where the few have total control over the many, wields sufficient enough power as to limit the possibility for future change. We must expose this for what it is before we fall into a political hole that we cannot escape.

COMMON SENSE Moment

The larger we grow the government, the smaller the private sector becomes.

Without the private sector creating the products, services and desirable tax paying jobs that generate the necessary income to run the government, the money needed to pay for all of these entitlements will begin to dry up and leave us with a less than motivated society that is used to handouts rather than earning a living and advancing one's self based on skill and determination.

All of the stimulus money that has been handed out recently is already taking affect. We have millions of workers who have dropped out of the workforce or failed to return to work after the pandemic.

Many of these people continue to get handouts in the form of unemployment insurance, food stamps, welfare, child credits based on the number of children you have and free Healthcare.

Most **Americans** would be shocked to know just how significant some of these handouts are in certain parts of the country.

Unemployment insurance was created to provide a helping hand to our citizens that found themselves out of work. It was never intended to replace one income with another but to provide a small stipend that filled the gap until they found a new job.

No one could live on their unemployment check for any long period of time nor should they be able to.

That was true for all of the social programs that we generated over the years. No one enjoyed their life under food stamps or welfare but they were there to help until they, hopefully, got a good job and raised themselves out of poverty.

Today, a family of four in certain states can actually collect as much as $75-80,000 per year is government assistance combined. That would place them way above the poverty line with funds equaling or surpassing their previous wages.

Are you surprised that many people who fall into this category have decided not to look for a job?

In the past, unemployment insurance lasted for a number of weeks and required those collecting checks to be looking for a job and to report on their efforts in order to keep receiving payments.

Today, the government has increased the unemployment checks with stimulus bonuses that add hundreds of dollars to the checks.

In addition, they have chosen to expand the weeks significantly to, in some cases, nearly a year, while at the same time removing the work requirement from the equation. Is anyone surprised that many workers have decided to stay home instead of trying to earn a living?

That is why today, thanks to an explosion of these programs beyond their original intention, a worker's motivation to succeed is taking a back seat to these handouts.

We have more job openings than we have workers willing to work. As far as I know, this has never happened before in this country.

How can our nation thrive and maintain their elite status on the world stage if our people refuse to work or lose their creative desires to succeed and excel in society?

If you are a **Progressive**, individual accomplishments and self motivation are not attributes that concern you at all. In fact, they frighten you.

Self worth is paramount to a person's belief that they are free to choose and free to live their life as they see fit. That does not compute in a **Socialist** or **Marxist** society.

The **Democratic Party** has always been the party of big government and social change. They have always felt that those in charge could manage your money better than you could and that the average **American** would squander their funds if not for the government providing for their well being.

That made the **Democratic Party** the perfect place for the **Progressive** movement to thrive and prosper.

All the **Progressives** needed to do was to place the big government policies of the **Democratic Party** on steroids and they were off to the races.

Their need to use deception rather than truth to express their beliefs were not just for the benefit of those on the other side of the aisle. They needed to hide their true agenda from the moderates in their own party, who would not be happy with a move toward **Socialism.**

The ultimate goal, we all know, is **POWER**. The more they control the less resistance they will encounter to their far left ideology.

James Madison understood how power can lead us down a path of destruction. Our Founding Fathers were careful to protect our newly form country from a Federal Government that thought their power was absolute when he said:

"If men were angels, no government would be necessary. If angels were to govern men, neither external nor internal controls on government would be necessary. In framing a government which is to be administered by men over men, the great difficulty lies in this: you must first enable the government to control the governed; and in the next place, oblige it to control itself."

The reasons for the failures of these **Marxist** principles over the past decades and centuries has a lot to do with the tremendous toll they take on those without the power.

The fact that government has never run anything very well nor fiscally sound provides insight into why these policies never seem to succeed.

When the masses in a S**ocialist** or M**arxist** society start to feel the pinch and begin to realize that they are powerless to do anything to change their fate, the protests begin in earnest.

The inevitable outcome of having robbed the people of their opportunities, including a means to defend themselves, finally hits home.

That's when the P**rogressives** in charge drop the hammer and remove the mask of concern to be replaced with the mask of compliance, one that exerts power over reason and they never take the mask off again.

The **Progressive** movement in **America** understands all of this and are well aware of its own history around the world.

By eliminating resistance and removing all stopgaps that can limit their power politically, they begin the destruction of our **Republic** and place all of us in great jeopardy.

We cannot sit back and allow this to happen.

Every American has the **COMMON SENSE** gene that needs to be resurrected from the deep recesses of their mind and placed, once again, front and center in their consciousness.

It is the responsibility of every patriot to expose the **Progressive** game plan and stop its advancement before it permeates our entire existence.

In order to do that, we first have to understand their playbook and put together our own game plan.

On the plus side, we are nowhere near the end of the game. The **Progressive** may have scored a few points early on but there is plenty of game left to play.

CHAPTER THREE

The Woke Culture

The concept of **WOKE** pretends to be the modern ramblings of concerned citizens that believe in replacing outdated language and principles with a new, updated version that is more inclusive and more socially acceptable.

Nothing could be farther from the truth.

In my opinion, it's a necessary tool in the **Progressive** arsenal that will further divide us as a nation and begin the breakdown of societal norms that will allow them to transform **America** with less resistance and more acceptance, two attributes that they hope will lead us down the road from a **Free Society** to one of **Social Dependency.**

Acceptance

In order to get us to accept their skewed view of who **America** is, they need to break down our natural resistance to change. That is a daunting task that requires substantial support from multiple fronts.

The **Progressives** already have a key support group in the **Media**. Through the **Media**, the **Progressives** can twist facts to distort their real message which might not be received well on face value.

The **Media** can also suppress the real truth when spinning can no longer hide the message by using their most powerful weapon, the power of **Omission**.

When twisting facts to fit your needs can no longer fool anyone, pretend that it does not exist at all.

Here are just some of the false or misleading beliefs that are constantly being presented as facts by our partisan **Media**:

- **The riots in the summer of 2020 were mostly peaceful.**
- **Black Lives Matter stands up for the Black Minority that have always been placed in a secondary role in America and remains so to this day.**
- **Our country is Systematically Racist and has been since the first slaves arrived at our door in 1619.**
- **All law enforcement has, and continues to be, systematically Racist in their actions and in their approach to justice.**
- **White Supremacy is prevalent in our society and stems primarily from the political right white population who are responsible for the continued racist actions that is part of who we are since the beginning of our nation.**
- **Racism is a one sided issue. It can only exist when a minority is undermined and subjugated by the white majority.**
- **The attack on January 6th, 2021 at the Capital was an insurrection carried out by white supremacist on the right that threatened the overthrow of our government.**

(The Media chose to ignore the fact that the rioters had no weapons and made no attempt to force their will on anyone once they made it into the Capital, making this the worst insurrection in world history, if we are to believe the charges.)

- **Outward expressions of patriotism, such as our Pledge of Allegiance and our National Anthem, carry less significance than previously thought. We live in a global world today and expressions of Nationalism are less desirable because it suggests that we are more important than every other nation on the planet.**

There was a time decades ago when you could trust the **Media** to provide you with the facts, not opinion.

I, for one, never knew the political leanings of **Walter Cronkite**, one of the most trusted people in journalism. He left the use of spin to the pundits who did that for a living and just reported the news.

Today, we can't seem to find an actual journalist amid a sea of pundits who, to our dismay, attempt to pass themselves off as journalists, knowing all too well that their deception might convince their followers that they are stating facts, rather than opinions.

It is difficult to get your opinions across to the masses when you have a voice that differs from that of the **Progressives**. The outright attacks and attempts to misquote the voices not towing the **Progressive** line are numerous and constant.

When did we evolve from a nation that fostered different opinions on key subjects to a nation that finds any opinion that differs from that of the powerful elite to be dangerous and not worthy of utterance?

When the **Media** cannot find a way to discredit you or twist your words to their advantage, they choose **OMISSION** as if your point never existed or was too insignificant to justify a comment.

When **President Trump** called the **Media** the bearers of **FAKE NEWS**, he was ridiculed and slammed harder than anyone in history.

They had no choice but to attack him with both barrels blasting. They could not let the public find out that he was telling the truth about how biased the information they were reporting was and their motives behind it.

There could be plenty of criticism of **President Trump,** from his constant tweeting to his less than presidential demeanor on occasion, but his refusal to accept the attacks that were directed his way without a fight, allowed the rest of us to finally see the main stream **Media** for the pretenders they were, bias to a fault and promoters of a particular point of view.

How the Covid-19 Pandemic was used to advance the Progressive Movement

The **Progressives** received a surprise gift when the world was attacked by a new viral infection that proved to be unrelenting as it spread among the masses with deadly consequences.

I am not suggesting that they were pleased by the impact it had on the global economy or the deadly toll it has and continues to take, but the reaction to the virus by governments and citizens alike suggested to the **Progressives** that there was a window of opportunity for them to solidify their **Social Agenda.**

How can they accelerate their push for **Social Change** without hitting a brick walk of resistance?

The secret lies in creating **FEAR** among our citizens, which could be manipulated by them to justify the second part of their plan to transform **America; Division** among the ranks.

FEAR

You can accomplish a great deal when your audience is driven more by **fear** than logic.

Because of the **fear** of the unknown, which was prevalent in the early stages of the pandemic, **America** agreed to shut down the most successful economy in our history in order to protect its citizens.

A **15 day** attempt at flattening the curve of infection and its impact on our healthcare system turned into a two year battle that left us with economic damage that no one could have foreseen.

Even today, while we have learned a great deal about the virus and its numerous variants, we still are being ruled by **fear**, thanks to the **Progressive** influence on our present **Administration**.

Remember what the tools of the **Progressive** movement are as they attempt to transform our country. When the facts are not on your side, turn to **Fear** and **Division.**

If you do not believe that we have created unimaginable **fear** in our citizens over the virus, just think how often you see a lone driver in his or her car wearing a mask.

How often we see people of all ages, including children, walking outside in the fresh air wearing masks in states where it is not required.

These are not logical measures based on everything we know but **fear** can replace **Common Sense** in many of us and lead to action that can only be described as extreme.

Right from the beginning, the **Progressives**, supported by the **Media**, backed the **FEAR** mantle and rode it on a daily basis.

They posted the infection numbers and the death numbers on TV screens daily and, even though we new little about the virus in the early days, they chose to verbalize the **FEAR** aspects and downplay the ever growing collection of **Facts** that was beginning to accumulate.

The **Facts** suggested that the elderly were more at risk, especially if they had a number of added morbidity triggers such as obesity, respiratory issues, heart issues, etc. While the **Media** did publicize these facts, they were on page two or three and it was the infections and deaths, without the details on page one.

As we went along in the early months and the number of infections increased significantly as the number of deaths increased at a slower pace, anyone with a calculator could do the math and see that **99% of** the infected population was surviving the virus.

Even narrowing the numbers to infected people over **65** years old, the death toll increased marginally with approximately **95%** of the infected surviving.

This was an opportunity for the **Media** to paint a less than dire picture of the risks going forward but that was not how they chose to react.

We heard horrible stories of parents and grandparents dying alone in nursing homes while their offspring mourned from afar.

While these stories were true and our overreacting to the virus separated families needlessly, in my opinion, those that passed away, for the most part, were still the most vulnerable and at higher risk.

How come there were no stories of the millions of people who contracted the virus, some of which were hospitalized and still managed to survive?

How come we never heard about the impact on our younger population, including hundreds of thousands of our citizens, who contracted the virus with minor symptoms, or on some cases, **NO** symptoms?

Division

As for creating the necessary **division** needed for real change, that was easy when dealing with the pandemic. Just demonize anyone who chooses to play loose with the rules, including States that refused to close down or demand total compliance.

The **Progressives** put immediate pressure on their **Democratic** base, to continue to force their citizens to follow the more restrictive measures. The desire to control and to maintain power became more important than the economic stability of their economy.

The Appearance of the Vaccines

Thanks to the previous president's **WARP SPEED** program, we managed to secure a number of vaccines years ahead of schedule, allowing the country to begin a campaign to protect the population from this deadly virus sooner rather than later.

While it appears that these vaccines have morphed into something resembling a flu shot where it helps with the severity rather than prevention, they are still beneficial, especially with our seniors who can suffer the most from an infection.

All of this was treated as **GOOD NEWS** and resulted in a significant portion of our population getting the vaccine and giving themselves a fighting chance in dealing successfully with a **Covid-19** infection.

The concern the **Progressives** had with the vaccines, in my opinion, centered on the possibility that **HOPE** might replace **FEAR** and that **UNITY** could overcome **DIVISION.**

That needed to change if they were to continue their push to soften all **Americans** to the idea of transforming our government toward

Socialism. They found their answer by using the vaccinations as a weapon rather than a tool.

The Vaccinated verses the Unvaccinated - The ultimate Division

While keeping the **Fear Factor** on steroids as they pushed for total vaccination, they found their enemy in the small portion of the country that resisted getting jabbed. Here lies the **Division** they so desire.

It became a war between both factions. The **Vaccinated** were the good guys who chose to protect their fellow **Americans** and the **Unvaccinated** were the bad guys who were putting the rest of their fellow **Americans** in danger of losing their lives.

It was the ideal battle of good versus evil with **American** against **American**. The **Progressives** had their war and they could not be more pleased with the opportunity to advance their agenda.

Anyone that turned to the main stream **Media** for their news could not miss the message being sent. You must get vaccinated or else you are risking the lives of every **American,** including your own.

The **Progressives** always understood that they needed **Americans** to be compliant with their demands if they were to succeed in transforming the country.

The use of **Fear** as a motivator is not new. When your safety and the safety of your family are threatened, there is very little you will not do to remedy things and keep everyone safe.

Why do criminals use guns during robberies? Why do kidnappers choose family members as hostages when demanding anything of importance from their chosen targets?

When given choices that involve death or injury to one's person or a loved one, chances of getting total cooperation from your victim is guaranteed, not just expected.

The **Progressives** took notice from the early stages of the pandemic and decided that this could work to their advantage.

The only questions that was left unanswered in their minds was how long could they maintain a high level of **Fear** and an unreasonable level of **Compliance** among our citizens?

We are now going on two years of our lives with the pandemic still part of the landscape and the possibility that the virus may be with us, like the Flu, for years to come.

During these past two years, many things have happened and we have learned a great deal about the virus and the dangers associated with the virus, that should have put many of us in a less anxious state. Unfortunately, the **Media** has done little to diminish our **Fears**.

The **Progressives** are well aware that the unknown always leads to a higher degree of anxiety. The longer they can leave many of the issues involving the virus unresolved or tenuous at best, the longer they can maintain a higher level of anxiety.

- **Why are we still suffering such emotional distress from the virus to the level where we see danger around every corner?**
- **Why have we not found a way to successfully treat the symptoms so as to allow us to get back to our normal lives?**
- **Why are too many of our citizens still living in fear and afraid to go out the door without some form of protection?**

The answers to those questions lie with our present **Progressive** leaders refusing to allow our citizens to see the light at the end of the tunnel.

The pandemic has allowed them to control us to a degree they thought impossible before the arrival of the virus. That level of power and influence is too important to their long range plans to abandon their focus and permit a return to normalcy.

The pandemic showed the **Progressives** a way to control **Americans** to do their bidding. The thought of letting go of control is not something they are willing to do.

Until they come up with a better way of accomplishing that objective, the virus will have to do and **Americans** will have to remain in fear.

To this day, most of the **States** that have burdened their citizens with the more egregious restrictions are still operating under the **Emergency Powers Act** which granted them control over their citizens not normally permitted by law.

When you taste unlimited power, it is hard to give it back.

The following **COMMON SENSE** moments regarding the pandemic are important tools in addressing the false narratives that have been broadcasted as truths by the M**edia** and the **Progressive** politicians.

We need to use these to awaken the more moderate, independent liberals to the fact that they have been lied to by a **Democratic Party** that no longer resembles the party of John F. Kennedy, or for that matter, William Clinton.

Remember what I said earlier. Arguing from a political point of view will fall on deaf ears. Using **Common Sense** and logic, with no political spin, might succeed in getting through to those that favor moderation.

It is time to say goodbye to the **Silent Majority**.

Common Sense Moments #1 (Pandemic)

The historical perspective on viruses and past pandemics suggest that reaching a level of HERD IMMUNITY is critical for eliminating potential hosts for the virus, eventually leading to its demise.

We were told early on by our medical professionals the same thing. The sooner we could reach 70-75% of our population having successfully survived the virus and having built up their own natural immunity, the virus would begin to run out of hosts and would eventually die off.

What happened to the benefit of natural immunity?

Why has our government totally ignored the more than ONE HUNDRED MILLION citizens that have contracted the virus and survived?

Why are we being told that a manufactured Vaccine is the only way for us to accumulate anti-bodies to fight off the virus?

What the heck has happened to the concept of HERD IMMUNITY?

Why was it the ONLY way for us to control the virus when we did not have the vaccines and now it appears to have NO value whatsoever?

If anyone has logical answers for these questions, we would love to hear them. If you cannot come up with any, then you need to ask yourself the really big question that hangs over the entire issue: **WHY?**

Why is our government and our medical advisors with the **CDC (Center for Disease Control)** and the **NIH (National Institute of**

Health) continuing to ignore the immunity that comes with having contracted the virus?

Combining everyone that has received the vaccination with everyone that has survived the virus, we are well above the original established parameters for **HERD IMMUNITY**. Isn't this what we were told needed to happen in order for us to begin to see the end of the pandemic and get our lives back to normal?

How come we are not celebrating our level of success?

If the reason is what I suspect it is, which is not wanting the issue to go away, then that level of deception borders on criminal negligence and deserves contempt.

The next step is to ask yourself why does the M**edia NEVER** ask the politicians or the medical professionals these questions directly nor demand a response without deflection?

The reason has to be a fear that the answers will fall short of credible, leaving them exposed to scrutiny, something they must avoid at all cost.

There is nothing about these questions that has to do with politics. You need to ask everyone, no matter their political leanings these questions and see what answers you receive.

If they are lacking in credibility or substance, then that is a conversation worth having and maybe, just maybe, we can shine a light on the deception that is the **Progressive** agenda.

Remember, we are not trying to create additional followers to our personal political beliefs. We are trying to expose the **Progressive Movement** for what it is.

A **Socialized America** will no longer be a country to look up to and admire. It will be a country on the verge of chaos and anarchy, no longer the "Shining City on the Hill."

Our **Republic** has survived for centuries and has prospered beyond our **Founding Fathers** expectations because of its limited government philosophy and its belief that **Freedom** was at the core of its existence.

Now, all of a sudden, are we to believe that we have been doing it all wrong and we need to change in order for us to be true members of a new global society that believes in less individual freedom and more collective thought?

I think not.

Common Sense Moment #2 (Pandemic)

We were told that once we received the vaccine we would have enough anti-bodies in our system to prevent us from contracting the virus.

Not only would we be protected, we would not be able to spread the virus to others and that was the only way for us to destroy the virus once and for all through 100% of the population getting vaccinated.

We have since learned that the present strain of the virus, the Omicron Strain, has managed to infect everyone, including the vaccinated. In addition, vaccinated citizens, even those that have received boosters to reinforce their immunity, are able to transmit the virus to others, both vaccinated and unvaccinated.

Why are we still proceeding with vaccine mandates in certain states and requiring everyone, from the age of 5 and up, to get their shot or put the rest of us in danger when we now know that the vaccine does not protect us or our fellow citizens from contracting the virus?

Why are our politicians still insisting that this is a pandemic of the unvaccinated?

Why are we continuing to demonize the unvaccinated as if

they are killing fellow citizens through their negligence and must be stopped?

Why are we still demanding mask mandates in certain states even though our medical professionals have already determined that the non-medical masks do not work well enough to protect anyone?

Maintaining the **Fear** and fostering the need for government control, under the guise of safety, is paramount to the **Progressive** plan of altering the **America** we have come to love.

Part of that is to maintain **Division** by continuing to demonize a portion of our population, amounting to millions of our brethren, by ignoring their reasons for remaining unvaccinated.

This is not purely ideological, since thousands of **Americans** have lost their jobs over this, destroying families and their means of support in the process.

Without the implied **Fear** that has been established over the virus, I doubt many **Americans** would tolerate this treatment, thus the need for the **Fear**, and its partner in crime **Division**, to continue indefinitely.

Who knows how far they may be able to carry on with the Fear?

If the **Progressives** can maintain the sense of dread all the way to the 2022 mid-term elections, maybe they can justify some of the same tactics that worked so successfully for them during the 2020 elections, such as mass mailings of ballots and loose verification of voter identity.

The real answers lie in the desire for **Power** and **Control**.

The **Progressives** are not pursuing this matter because they have legitimate concerns over the virus and its potential impact on **American** citizens.

They must find a way to have total control over our lives and the path the country will take to their promised land of total **Social Control**.

They do not care about any of us on a personal level. They just see us as a collective that can be managed in such a way as to allow them to take over just about everything of importance.

Using the pandemic to their advantage is only one of their weapons in the toolbox.

The more diverse their assault on our freedoms, the better the chance that such diversity leads to less clarity on our part.

COMMON SENSE MOMENT #3 - (The Chinese Connection)

Everyone is aware of the brutal attacks by the Media on our former President.

One of those attacks that were relentless involved his continued use of the term "China Virus". The Media hated it and they made no bones about letting the rest of us know how much they despised the message.

The Media criticized him at every turn and went so far as to attach a racial reason behind his use of the term.

At one point, when there was an uptick in violent Asian crime in our country, they went so far as to suggest that his demonization of China was the prime reason why a number of his followers were behind the recent violence against Asian Americans.

While the issue of blame quietly went away when the videos started to appear showing many of these crimes being carried out by African Americans, who were not considered a part of his base supporters, there were no apologies or retractions from the Media, just silence.

The real crime, in my opinion, resulted from the Progressives

opposition to anything Trump, which led to their supporters and the Media giving China a pass on this issue for no other reason than Trump was doing the opposite.

That was a major mistake as China was not only responsible for the virus, they allowed it to spread to the world without restraint.

China began by claiming that the virus was accidentally transmitted from a wet market in Wuhan where a number of exotic animals were sold.

They denied any connection to the viral lab that was minutes away and were adamant about not letting any of the world medical professionals in to examine the facility or assist them in identifying the cause.

They even tried blaming it on international travelers to China and American sailors but those claims fell on deaf ears.

While the world was dealing with a pandemic of untold proportions, most of the countries affected, including the United States, were upset with China and their refusal to assist in identifying the source, but not nearly outraged enough for the chain of events that led to the pandemic.

The Media's intent on attacking our President, along with Corporate America's dependence on China, led to an atmosphere of disappointment with China over their stubbornness to help solve the origin issue.

To say we totally missed the point, either accidentally or intentionally, would be an understatement.

Whether China accidentally released the virus due to a lab leak or whether they intentionally did so, though no one wants to go down that road, their actions were not only unforgivable but criminal.

While the world knew very little about what was going on in

Wuhan at the end of 2019 and the beginning of 2020, the Chinese government was well aware that they had a dangerous virus on their hands that was transmissible between humans and capable of causing serious illness and death.

The reason we know this is they isolated Wuhan from the rest of their mainland and prevented any travel to and from the region.

This was the perfect time for them to come clean to the rest of the world and put us on notice as to the potential dangers associated with the virus.

What China chose to do instead was criminal and intentional, opening the door to the question as to whether China decided to create a global pandemic that would ruin the world's economies or they inadvertently allowed it to escape. You notice I have not used the word accidental.

The benefits to China, by allowing a global economic fallout, especially in America where we were experiencing a level of growth that was unprecedented, was not out of the realm of possibility for a country that would steal any technology, use slave labor to lower their cost of goods or imprison anyone not towing the party line.

Here's where COMMON SENSE needs to take center stage.

When China first realized that the virus, no matter where it originated, was dangerous and infectious and could spread through their country with disastrous results, they closed down the city of Wuhan and isolated it from the rest of China in an effort to stop the spread of the virus in their country.

Those actions alone suggest they knew how dangerous the virus was.

Remembering that they were the only nation who knew about the virus and it's deadly potential, they then allowed residents of Wuhan to travel around the globe without any restrictions, guaranteeing that the virus would infect the rest of the world.

By choosing silence and deception over the needs of others, they became criminal accomplices to a crime of massive proportions and deserve worldwide condemnation.

Instead, they have received nothing more than a mild acknowledgment of the role they played in the pandemic, as if it was more a disappointment rather than an intentional act that led to worldwide casualties.

I, for one, will never intentionally buy another product manufactured in China if I can help it nor will I support any company that chooses to place their business interests in China ahead of America.

As for our political leaders, who chose to back China because Trump was adamantly opposed to their actions, they have exposed their true colors and would prefer this issue just goes away as we still, after two years, are dealing with China's intentional efforts to ruin our economy.

Make no mistake. In this country, we are at war with a **Progressive** ideology that can destroy our present way of life and take away our freedom to choose a different path.

Thomas Jefferson once said:

"If people let government decide what foods they eat and what medications they take, their bodies will soon be in as sorry a state as are the souls of those who live under tyranny."

Anyone who tries to pretend that a war with the **Progressive Movement** is a war between **Democrats** and **Republicans**, is missing the mark entirely.

We need both parties to be viable and healthy in order to maintain a vibrant political landscape where different opinions and approaches to governing can be challenged and debated for the good of the **American** people.

The fault lies with anyone believing that the **Progressive Movement** is a legitimate representation of the **Democratic Party**.

While many **Democrats** might be comfortable with government having more control over key issues, I doubt they would like total control over all issues of importance to the detriment of our basic freedoms, which is the goal of **Progressivism.**

This is a war we cannot afford to lose.

To defeat this enem**y** we will need good people from both parties to see the light and reject **Socialism** as an acceptable political replacement for **Capitalism**.

CHAPTER FOUR

Control the Language and You Control the Narrative

Progressivism

On the surface, this sounds like a positive, upbeat word that describes ones ability to move forward or evolve from a previous position to a better, more enlightened one.

Isn't it better to be **progressive** rather than stagnant? After all, no one progresses from a position of strength to one of weakness. When going in the wrong direction you would use other words or phrases, such as declining or taking a step backwards, never progressing.

All of us who have voted in national elections are well aware that there are a number of candidates on the ballot that we know nothing about.

Usually, they can range from the **Green Party** all the way to the **Communist Party**, with multiple parties in between.

While most of us believe that none of these candidates have any chance of winning the election, they still represent ideological movements that manage to get enough backing as to get their names on the ballot.

If the **Progressives** chose to call themselves the **Socialist Party** or the **Marxist Party**, names that better describe their political ideology, the negative connotation such names infer would end their dream before it began.

That is why they prefer deception to outright exposure. The language needs some tweaking if it is to work to their benefit.

I'm sure that many of our citizens who remain loyal to the **Democratic Party,** have no idea that a significant number of their political leaders are leaning toward **Socialism** rather than **Capitalism,** not just the obvious players like **AOC** or **Bernie Sanders**.

There are millions of **Democrats** out there, in my opinion, that need to take a more critical eye to those in their party that pretend to be looking out for their best interests.

While your heart may be in the right place and aligned with **Democratic** leaders of the past, you are not being shown the truth. The **Progressive Movement** is a lot more than just a slight slide to the left.

If the **Progressives** manage to take over the entire **Democratic Party,** we will no longer have a two party system that provides the necessary **Checks and Balances** that help to make **America** the country everyone else looks up to for guidance and support.

The language does matter.

Nationalism

I have no idea when this word became something to loathe rather than embrace.

It probably began when our previous president made no bones about his **America First** approach to governing and how important it was to him.

There is no doubt that technology has brought the entire planet to our door almost instantaneously. Most of our larger corporations are truly global in stature and they have taken a less than nationalistic approach to their business.

In fact, many of our prominent politicians on both sides of the aisle have been getting campaign donations and gathering influence on an international scale for years, making them less likely to burn any bridge that may turn off the faucets of financial support.

It should come as no surprise that many in **Corporate America** would prefer that we take a more **Global** approach to everything. Even the hint of an **America First** stance could appear to be threatening to their interests, especially since their bottom line has international repercussions.

In order to combat both the president they despised and the message itself, the **Media** decided to condemn the term and pretend that it represented a selfish approach to world affairs that ignored the rest of the world in favor of our own self interests.

Nothing could be further from the truth.

We are the most powerful and most benevolent nation on the planet because of our **Nationalistic** approach, not in spite of it.

Try and find another country that would put the needs of their people behind the needs of others and I will show you a country that is in decline.

Everyone must get their house in order before they can branch out. Believing in maintaining a healthy **America** does not mean the rest of the world be damned.

To demonize **Nationalism** is to deny **Patriotism** as well as the belief that **American** superiority is actually good for the rest of the world.

The **Progressives** will not succeed if **Patriotism** and our independent freedoms remain high on our list of priorities.

A good place to start is to begin with word games and that includes turning **Nationalism** into something bad.

Equity and Equality

The **Progressives** throw the word **Equity** around like candy.

They know perfectly well that using that word and pretending that it is a good thing, no matter the context, can help them sway public opinion. After all, **Equity** is just another word for **Equality**, is it not?

Equality, as we all know, comes right out of our **Constitution** and is the basis for who we are and what we strive to be.

Everyone is equal in this country and deserves to be treated fairly and on equal footing no matter their race, gender or economic status.

When our ancestors drifted away from the initial foundation created by our **Founding Fathers**, it took a war of untold proportions to bring the country back into the fold and begin both the healing process and the difficult task of establishing **Equality** for all in our country.

This did not happen overnight nor are we ever going to achieve perfection in that regard but we should never stop working toward the goal of true **Equality** for everyone in this country.

In short, **Equality** provides equal opportunity to all under the law. Everyone is free to choose their own path and not be encumbered with obstacles that are not in the way of every **American**, no matter their race, gender or religious beliefs.

Equity is not the same, no matter what the **Media** and the **Progressives** want you to believe.

Equity, as it is being used by the **Progressives,** says that each and every person has the right, not to the same opportunities as everyone else but the same outcomes, which is counter to everything we believe and strive for in **America**.

When we are talking about rights rather than individuals, **Equity** is a good thing.

For example, every person has the right to invest in the market and are only limited by the funds they choose to invest. When profits and losses are calculated, we do not tolerate **WHITE** investors getting a higher return on their investment than a **MINORITY** investor because of their skin color. Everyone understands that.

In Healthcare, for example, every person who has a health policy, no matter their race, gets equitable treatment under the policy for themselves and their family. No one gets a better deal for the same policy because of their race or gender.

When the **Progressives** talk about **Equity**, they are practicing a form of reverse **racism** when they demand equal outcomes based on race and gender.

The school system is a prime example of how they are trying to create division among us.

When you begin to alter tests and change grading so that students with lower grades are not stigmatized for their failures, under the guise of **Equity**, you are doing more to hurt the top producers, who no longer are lauded for their efforts, than you are providing help to the rest of the students.

This is nothing short of insane.

Some schools are eliminating accelerated classes for advanced students because it leaves the average and below average student behind, which makes them feel sad and unhappy.

What about the advanced student that is looking to excel so that they can take advantage of their exceptional intellect to move ahead?

This is, most likely, the group of individuals that will produce our future scientists, future doctors and future entrepreneurs who will keep **America** successful and prosperous. Should we prevent them from advancing in order to cater to those with less noticeable skills?

Other schools are looking to drop grading entirely so as not to embarrass the poor performing students who do not measure up to the better students.

Why do they refuse to acknowledge that many of the underperforming students might just not be applying themselves to the best of their ability?

How does **Race** play into this?

The **Progressives** promote **Equity** under the false notion that higher educational standards favor a White Majority to the detriment of Black and Hispanic Minorities.

It is my opinion that this is just another form of **Racism**. I would like to think that minorities would find this insulting to think they lack the ability to keep up with the other students.

There are many reasons that some inner city schools perform worse than others. None of those reasons include the lack of ability or intelligence on the part of the student.

To suggest otherwise is nothing short of **Soft Racism** and the **Progressives** need to be called out for it.

In the grand scheme of things for the **Progressives**, this is another form of dependency, which is a critical step toward acceptance.

Make the below average performers believe that their failings are not their fault but the fault of society and its rigged system and you have started the road to dependency for millions of Americans who prefer having someone or something else be to blame for their failings.

This is a dangerous game they are playing when we no longer need drive and determination to excel as a motivator. What happened to the old adage of putting in the work and reaping the rewards?

Common Sense Moment

Equity, as it is being promulgated by the Progressives, remains a dangerous tool that can only lead to more division and a greater loss of trust. We must learn to identify it for what it is and point it out when we see it.

The worst thing for our minority citizens to do is to fall into the trap of believing that they cannot succeed because of who they are, what color their skin is or where they live.

When we fail to try, we succeed at failing. When the government tells us that we cannot succeed because of intangible things such as race and gender, we lose faith in ourselves and fall into the trap of depending on others for just about everything.

I cannot think of a sadder set of circumstances than when our citizens no longer try to succeed but choose to accept their present condition as being a lifelong burden.

We must keep in mind what the ultimate goal of the Progressive movement is when looking through the prism of their many deflections that are disguised as social justice issues. By constantly asking ourselves WHY they need to deflect the truth, we can begin to answer that for ourselves.

The truth, if presented without their spin and deflection, would not be accepted kindly by most Americans.

Freedom loving patriotic Americans would never accept Socialism or Marxism as a way of life if they understood the sacrifices they were going to have to make and the loss of freedoms they were going to have to endure.

Democracy and Republic are NOT Synonymous

Have you ever noticed that the **Progressives** in power never use the term **Republic**? They continue to call us a **Democracy.**

Our **Founding Fathers** understood that we needed to be a lot more than just a **Democracy**.

In fact, **Thomas Jefferson** understood all too well why **America** needed to be more than just a Democracy in order to survive and prosper when he said:

"Democracy is nothing more than mob rule, where fifty-one percent of the people may take away the rights of the other forty-nine."

When we played games as a child on the street, **Democracy** worked well, though not without its objections.

When a bunch of us kids wanted to play punchball while others preferred playing stickball, we voted. The majority always won even though complaints from the losers were less than civil on occasion.

Democracy is a great thing and needs to be preserved but running a massive country that spreads out for thousands of miles, and hundreds of millions of **Americans**, requires a system that recognizes and rewards such diversity of thought and circumstance.

As we all know, the **Progressives** have most of their supporters among the highly populated cities across the country. These population bases benefit most from the funds coming from our government assistance programs.

In other words, they benefit the most from cradle to grave entitlements that stifle creativity and limit personal motivation to both succeed beyond the government and take advantage of opportunities to alter ones social standing.

Unfortunately, these large population centers house a great many

Americans and can significantly influence elections by their sheer numbers, if permitted to do so, thus the need for a **Republic** rather than a **Democracy.**

You see, the ultimate **POWER** in a **Republic** is held by the people, not their representatives. The goal is to have the citizens in control with their elected officials doing the bidding, not the other way around.

It is going to take a miracle for a **Republican** to run **California** anytime soon, in spite of the fact that the majority of counties in the state are more moderate, even conservative in their philosophy.

While the geographic breakdown favors the moderate views, the population base does not. If the moderate candidate wins every county in the state, with the exception of the counties surrounding Los Angeles, San Francisco, Oakland and Sacramento, they will still lose the election.

That is why the **Progressives** would love to eliminate the **Electoral College**, which allows **ALL** of the country to have a voice in national elections.

Without the safeguards that protect the votes of Middle America, the cities of Los Angeles, New York, Chicago, Boston and Newark could easily cancel the moderate voices and virtually eliminate the two party system that has served us well for more that two hundred years.

We need **EVERY** State in the nation and every **American** to have a say in who will represent them. Without proper representation being recognized through the **Electoral College,** the cities and the surrounding communities would be in charge of our national elections not the whole of the nation.

As you have probably noticed, I choose not to use the term **Democrat,** to describe the political party in power, that often. I'm not really sure just how many **Democrats**, in the traditional sense of the word, still exists.

The takeover of one of our proud political parties by the far left

Progressive Movement has been shocking, to say the least, in its dominance and the mercurial speed with which they have come to prominence.

I still believe that our country of more than **330** million people are a lot more balanced than one might expect from the actions of the **Progressives**. As a whole we are closer to left center and right center than we are to the extreme of either party.

Because the country tends to lean toward the middle, the **Progressives** and their **WOKE** movement have taken the language mantel to heart and ran with it.

Any language that they consider to be threatening or that might reinforce principles that remind **Americans** of who they are and where their values originated, must be either eliminated or tossed on the pile of irrelevancy.

One of the those words is the term **Republic**.

Rather than trying to make the point that **Democracy** (majority rules) is better for the country than a **Republic** (every **American** has a say, no matter where they reside), they choose to ignore the word or to pretend both words mean the same.

The Progressive War on Christianity

This is not a new attack. **Christians** have been dealing with this assault for decades. The attempts to rid **God** from our schools, our **Pledge of Allegiance** and even our money have been going on since the late 70's.

When you understand the goals of the **Progressives** and the underlying attributes of **Christianity**, it makes perfect sense. They want total allegiance and dependency on the government while **Christian** values place **God** above everything else and teaches us that we need to **Love Our Neighbor as We Do Ourselves.**

The **Progressives** require that we pit neighbor against neighbor if they are to succeed in breaking down our core beliefs in freedom of thought and freedom of choice.

While we are a predominantly **Christian** nation, all religion is a threat to the **Secular Progressive Movement** and they need us to either abandon our attachments to religion or de-emphasize its importance in our lives so that the **State** can take its rightful place at the head of the table.

Because it plays an importance role in our lives, religion is in the crosshairs of the **WOKE** mob and a key enemy to the **Progressive Movement**.

We only have to look as far as the words of **Karl Marx** to better understand the **Progressive** stance on **Religion**:

"The first requisite for the happiness of the people is the abolition of Religion."

We are all aware of their war on **Christmas** over the years.

While they have not succeeded in winning that war, they have won a number of battles along the way and that is how they planned on fighting this war all along. The more battles won, the less resistance going forward.

Our schools have stopped allowing any religious content within their walls, even the desire to pray before or after a sporting event. Quite a few coaches have been admonished, and in a few cases fired, for taking a knee and thanking **God** after a game.

While they have yet to remove **God** from the **Pledge of Allegiance**, they have succeeded in getting a number of schools to stop saying the

Pledge during school hours. **God** help us if any teacher said a prayer or acknowledged a higher power for guidance.

During the pandemic, the government managed to classify grocery stores, big box stores, liquor stores, medical facilities and even tattoo parlors as essential businesses while churches needed to close and remain closed for the duration.

Some municipalities refused to allow **Pastors** and **Rabbis** to hold outdoor services even as they permitted outdoor dining. I guess only a religious service could qualify as a super spreader event.

What about allowing the churches to open using masks and sufficient space between the parishioners? Just shut up and obey was the universal response from **Progressives** running our Cities, States and Municipalities.

By choosing to protect the feelings and concerns of a minuscule portion of society who are offended by religious items or expressions, they have forced the majority to cower to their demands and to give up some of their freedoms in order to appease a handful of **Agnostics** who are really **Progressives** in disguise.

In other words, religious **Americans** will never permit anyone or any secular power to take a position of importance higher than their loved ones or their **God**.

The need for the **Progressives** to secularize **America** should be obvious.

COMMON SENSE MOMENT (Religion)

Does anyone truly believe that someone finds the mention of GOD on our dollar bills or the appearance of a statue of a saint in front of a municipal building as being so damaging to their existence as to require its removal?

Does anyone believe that just the mention of Christmas is so disturbing to someone that they had to force many of our companies, schools, entertainment venues, municipalities and government entities into abandoning the Christmas season in favor of a Holiday celebration that honors no one?

How many Agnostics are there in America? How many Americans are so non-religious as to warrant public outrage over the slightest expression of our religious beliefs?

That's where we make our mistake. We take the outrage of the very few and allow it to dictate our traditions and celebrations when it is nothing more than a ruse to further secularize our society.

Remember the discussion about the WOKE movement? A handful of basement dwellers with no viable social life can appear to be tens of thousands of outraged citizens when they use Social Media to their advantage.

The Progressives created the WOKE movement and continue to allow it to beat Americans into submission one issue at a time.

The more we permit them to attack, under the guise of tolerance for others, the more they pick away at us until we no longer feel the pain and just lose our desire to resist.

When that happens, the battles will end and the war will be lost. Its better to stand up now.

These are not small, inconsequential disagreements that we are dealing with that suggests to us that its better to turn the other cheek rather than take on a battle so insignificant.

Christians, as well as most Religious citizens, are a forgiving people who tend, as a whole, to give others the benefit of the doubt.

Their compassion and desire to help rather than hurt, is being used against them as they allow the **Progressives** to control the language and the issues from a confrontational position that demands compliance rather than suggesting compromise.

Its time for us to be a little less **Christian** and more immovable when it comes to letting the **Progressive** minority interfere with our core beliefs.

This brings us back to the M**edia** and their role in providing the informational support that the **Progressives** so desperately need to accomplish their mission.

Let's take a closer look at who they really are and how they are controlling the narrative to the detriment of the country.

The Media and its Role in our March Toward Socialism

The history of the **Media** in our country over the past few centuries has always centered on the need to educate the masses to the facts concerning any topic they deem important enough to communicate.

As for political matters, the **Media** knows that partisan members of both parties will continue to spew biased information that favors their point of view so as to influence the general population that their positions warrant support and unwavering acceptance.

To say that our experienced politicians are quite good at slanting the facts to fit their needs would be an understatement.

The need for the **Media** to objectively present the facts has been a critical part of our history and our culture.

Americans require unbiased reporting in order for them to sift through the muddled rantings of politicians. Who will safeguard each and every **American's** right to the facts, if not the **Media**?

It is my opinion that over the past half century, the **Media** has slowly abandoned their objective responsibility in favor of political bias and many **Americans**, even to this day, have failed to see the forest for the trees.

While there has been many examples of outright lies and untruths that have been presented as fact by the **Media**, the most damaging and nefarious breach of their responsibility to objectively present the facts has been the **sin of omission**.

While there are a limited number of **Media** websites and broadcast operations that offer a different point of view, they are few and far between.

The **Progressive** slant still dominates the marketplace for the less politically interested among us, providing a major pulpit to spread their philosophy, not as opinion or as another point of view, but as fact, making it appear to be unquestioned dogma. This is dangerous and misleading, to say the least.

However, pretending to be neutral when you're not is necessary when the true purpose of your message would not be received very well without the cover of deception.

Progressives conduct their communicative business in the arena of emotion, not fact, for the most part. The reason for this is obvious. **Facts** do not benefit their objectives.

The **Media** is the most dangerous when they **FAIL** to report the facts because they are indefensible. Here are a few examples of what I mean:

Example #1

- **Hunter Biden's laptop is full of damaging facts about himself, his family and their ability to generate millions**

of dollars based on having just one valuable skill at his disposal; the skill of influence.

- **Hunter can provide direct access to the President (formally the Vice-President) of the United States and it appears that he has used that skill to fill his coffers with an abundance of financial rewards.**

(It's important to state that the ownership and veracity of the laptop's contents have never been disputed successfully. In fact, The New York Times, a bastion of liberal thinking, has verified its authenticity, along with its contents. Believe me, if it was fake, we would all know it by now.)

Because of the damaging nature of this credible information and without a viable path to discredit its contents, the **Media** chose silence over reporting and, with the cooperation of the large tech companies, they kept the masses from learning any of this unless they took the initiative to search for it themselves.

The vast majority of the country are not active political enthusiasts. They are casual observers at best. In fact, few of them are news junkies at all.

What they know about the news of the day comes from headlines and television reports, none of which allowed this story to take hold with the exception of reporting early on how the intelligence community suspected the story to be **Russian** mis-information, a claim that was never verified.

When the **Progressives** and **Big Tech** chose lies and innuendoes rather than fact, the **Media** cooperated by killing the story altogether, leaving most of the nation clueless to the seriousness of the information on the laptop. They allowed a national election to take place under the cover of darkness.

Example #2

- **The United States ended their twenty year war in Afghanistan. The promise that we made to our citizens and Afghan allies that supported us over the last two decades was a promise of freedom for them and their immediate families with the proper exit visas if they chose to leave at the time of our departure.**

When it became apparent that the Taliban was taking over the country by force, the lives of all Americans in country and Afghan allies in particular, were in serious peril. Extraction was the only safe answer once terrorists were in control of the country.

While the majority of **Americans** agreed that the war had been going on too long and needed to end, how we chose to leave has been disastrous, though many **Americans** are unaware of the severity of what occurred, thanks to the **Media.**

They touted the **Administration's** talking points of how hundreds of thousands of refugees were rescued and evacuated from the country, forgetting the important details of how many **Americans** and tens of thousands of **Afghan Allies** and green card holders, who were promised sanctuary for their support of the United States, remained behind and in danger of losing their lives.

How many horror stories about the Taliban controlled **Afghanistan**, including death squads hunting for those supporters that were left behind, has made its way to the masses? Are there any actual stories being reported at all? It's as if this is old news and there is nothing to tell or report.

We still have hundreds of brave contractors in **Afghanistan** trying to get as many of these people out as possible. Neither their efforts nor the killings and hangings that are taking place throughout the country by the **Taliban Death Squads** are included in the evening news or on the pages of most newspapers across the country. The sin of **OMISSION** is the word of the day.

Because of the horrendous way our extraction from **Afghanistan** occurred, leaving billions of dollars worth of weapons, including military planes, helicopters and vehicles behind, it was impossible for the **Media** and the **Progressives** in government to hide many of the obvious faults in the extraction process.

This, in my opinion, was the start of the dramatic decline in popularity that presently exists for the **Administration** in general and **President Biden** in particular.

That did not stop them from deflecting the horrible loss of life and the failure to extract **ALL** of our citizens and supportive **Allies**, as being beyond anyone's control.

While this story could not be omitted from the news, the **Media** thought they could distract us from the real horrors that were occurring by pretending that we had succeeded in our mission to extract **Afghans** from the war zone.

The truth was that our failure to secure the city and the country by removing **ALL** of our military assets **BEFORE** we began the process, resulted in our enemies controlling the surrounding area, not us.

When thousands of **Afghans** charged the airport and created utter chaos, our government chose to evacuate many of them because of their proximity to the planes. The loss of control of the area prevented thousands of legitimate allies from making it to the airport at all, thus they were left behind.

The failure to successfully end our war in **Afghanistan** by leaving the country properly will be judged by historians, in my opinion, as one of the worst moments in our history.

Our failure to save many of our **Allies** from death and starvation at the hands of the Taliban will give many future **Allies** pause before trusting **America** to keep their word in return for assistance and cooperation.

Losing trust on the world stage cannot be understated. Thanks to our present leaders, that **Shining City on the Hill i**s less illuminated today than it was yesterday.

Common Sense Moment - Perception

If you want to know when you are being lied to and when there is a lack of factual evidence to defend a particular position by either the Progressives or the Media, notice the severity of their objections.

The level of outrage that follows any discourse that opposes their positions far outweigh the proper response. The more truth that the opposing view exposes, the greater the level of outrage.

When you cannot muster a sufficient amount of proof that Climate Change is a problem that requires us to reimagine our entire economy immediately, you choose to pretend that we are all going to die if we do not capitulate to their demands for change.

When you have an opposing view, such as that which is presented by the most successful cable news channel in the country in terms of number of viewers (FOX NEWS), it is not sufficient to just tell your audience that you have a different point of view. You need to rant and rave about the lies and arrogance of those who dare represent the channel or choose to listen to their broadcasts.

They cannot be just competitors, they need to be demonized as a blemish on society and a threat to Democracy. The greater the outrage, the less chance your listeners or readers will ever be tempted to sample their evil discourse.

Thanks to our present Media, we no longer have a platform for calm discord nor a platform for civil debate.

When our colleges and universities decide that they would rather boycott and protest anyone with a different opinion, they are going against the basic principles of education which requires understanding all points of view before choosing a side.

Why have none of the major Media outlets taken any of these students to task when they choose ignorance over debate? It's because they agree with the need to stifle opposing views rather than accept them.

As we have said before, the Progressives, with the support of the Media, hold positions that are indefensible as they lead us toward Socialism.

When you can't win an argument on facts, defuse it with emotion and bluster.

Maybe no one will notice that the truth, hidden behind the curtain, never sees the light of day.

CHAPTER FIVE

RACISM

Unfortunately, **Racism** exists just about everywhere and **America** is not immune from its influence.

I doubt that we will ever see the end of some form of **Racism** in **America,** no matter how hard we try.

When you have more than **300** million people that are free to believe in their own ideals, which include their own prejudices, you will have examples of every type of hatred that **MAN** can imagine.

We have progressed over the past few centuries from an era where slavery was commonplace, not only in **America**, but across the globe. The classification of certain races and cultures as being inferior and less deserving of common decency reflects a dark period that has no place in society and well deserving of the outrage and condemnation that has been cast upon it.

When studying history, one will find that **America** is among the more enlightened nations, having fought a long and bloody war in order to uphold the Constitution's core belief that **ALL Men Are Created Equal.**

Many **Americans,** post **Civil War,** may have been forced to accept the legal interpretation of the word **Freedom** but they resisted the primary requirement for a successful transition, the emotional acceptance that the directive was more than a collection of words. They still held on to their belief that one race was inferior, no matter what the law dictated, and acted accordingly.

It has taken decades of growth to significantly reduce the number of people choosing to live in the past. Those who would be classified as true **Racists** has declined significantly over the past decades and no matter what you are being told by the **Media** and the **Progressives**, just a fraction of our population still hold this belief.

Combating **Racism** may be a work in progress that will continue for quite some time but we are miles ahead of our past and we are successfully striving for equality in all aspects of our society, not just preaching its virtues.

Calling someone a **Racist** remains one of the more extreme and alienating charges that one could levy against another.

How that has changed over the past few decades has a lot to do with the **Progressive Movement** and their attempt at dividing our nation further in order to achieve their objectives.

It is a core requirement of the **Progressive** agenda to see **Racism** everywhere and under every rock. Only then can true division and hatred among fellow citizens be cultured and manipulated for their purposes.

Because of their overused claim of **Racism** in our society, the word has lost meaning and it no longer carries the stigma that it richly deserves. If everyone is **Racist**, then no one is **Racist**.

COMMON SENSE MOMENT - Racism

It is hard to look at America today and not be able to see, with our own eyes, how far we have come in the past half century regarding racial equality.

Our political landscape highlights the fact that minorities have successfully run for office on both a local and national level with significant success.

We have Representatives in Congress, both men and women of color, as well as a number of Senators.

Let's not forget that we have recently had our first minority President in our nation's history and presently have a minority Vice-President, who also happens to be a woman.

On a statewide level, it appears that many mayors and local politicians are minorities, making it difficult to believe that their race or skin color is holding them back from obtaining public office.

Let's not forget that in order to win a number of these elections, especially those on a national level, you need to garner support from the white majority or you will never succeed.

These minorities are in office because of the support they received from non-minority voters that the Progressives want you to believe are racist to their core.

The Entertainment Industry, which was years ahead of the rest of the country to begin with, does not reflect a shortage of minority performers to entertain us and serenade us with their talents.

The influence of minorities in Sports goes without saying. While there may be a few sports where minorities are less prevalent, it is not because they are prevented from participating.

In sports, anyone with the skill and talent to perform at a high level will be afforded the opportunity to do so, no matter their race or skin color.

Because of the progress we have achieved so far and the barriers that have been eliminated regarding race, it is difficult to accept the recent rants from the Progressives.

How they can insist that we, as a country, are not only trending

backwards toward a more racist period in our history, but we are SYSTEMICALLY Racist, a claim so horrible as to paint America as a country that is too far gone as to be beyond our efforts to ever achieve racial harmony. Can such a claim be true?

As with most of our Common Sense moments, we need to ask the question WHY?

Why is it necessary for the Progressives to point out that Racism not only exists in America but is so prevalent as to be beyond our control to address and combat? Could it be that they do not want to combat Racism at all?

If we are beyond repair, then the need to reimagine our country and its form of government is necessary in order to put the country back on track. The last thing the Progressives are looking to do is correct a situation that is manageable.

The answer to the question of Systemic Racism must be something that lies beyond the question itself.

In my opinion, the Progressives have no interest in Racism at all. They only want to use the issue to change our country into something that many of us will no longer recognize.

The **Progressives** choice of the word **Systemic** is a serious charge that they never seem to explain. If we are waiting for the **Media** to provide the necessary clarification for us, we are never going to get anywhere.

Systemic means that the entire entity, not just a localized or minor part of that entity, is infected to the point that the entity can no longer function free of its influence.

If true, **America**, as we know it, cannot be saved. We are too far gone. Luckily for us, the **Progressives** have a solution.

They believe we need to cut out the infected portion, which is fueled by **Capitalism**, similar to a surgeon removing a cancerous tumor. We can then replace the infected system with a more inclusive system known as **Socialism**. Only then will we be free of our **Racist** tendencies.

These are not new charges put forth by the **Progressives**. In the past, it was a small minority of extremist that proposed these far left ideals and disparaging remarks about how bad **America** was and how we needed to start by moving away from **Capitalism**, the bane of our existence.

Their unexpected rise to power within the present Administration has them accelerating their plans for a takeover now that they can see a window of opportunity that had previously been closed to their point of view.

COMMON SENSE MOMENT - The Only Question That Matters

We have already discussed how, in a country with a population in excess of 300 million, we can find examples of just about EVERY form of behavior that challenges our minds with both a sense of wonder and horror.

For every example of deviant and ungodly behavior, we can find acts of pure unselfishness and bravery, that leaves us feeling inadequate for our failure to rise to a similar level of commitment.

For every horrible example of violence, racism or inhumanity to man, we have another example of kindness and sacrifice that leaves us with a sense of pride and patriotism, confident that our nation is not beyond redemption.

If our country were truly Systematically Racist, every aspect of society would have been infiltrated with the sins of Racism and Bias, which would make it difficult for any minority to succeed

and prosper as society would have created barriers to prevent their advancement.

That leaves us with a very important question to ask of anyone that might believe we are losing the battle for Racial Equality. Can they think of one law that is in place that is restricting minorities from advancing and succeeding in America?

Is there anything tangible that you can point to that illustrates how our Systemically Racist nation has placed legal barriers in the way of anyone trying to succeed, no matter their race, gender, skin color or religious affiliation?

This is why the Progressives always deal with emotion rather than fact. The facts are never on their side.

They take isolated examples of racism and prejudice and pretend that these tiny samples of bad behavior are a reflection on our entire society. That's how they try to bludgeon us to death with claims of racism, transphobia, gender bias, religious intolerance, etc.

If America were a Systematically Racist nation, our laws and our system of justice would be filled with obstacles and faintly disguised prejudices that interfere with the rights of minorities.

Their claim is unwarranted and lacking in evidence but that only matters if the Media and our fellow citizens demand accountability. Silence is the same as acceptance.

The Media will never voice objection but our fellow Americans better decide to be that voice before we begin to lose the will to do so.

Today, the playbook has changed and now favors the **Progressives**. When our own **President** is telling us that our country is **Systemically Racist**, we cannot choose to dismiss it so quickly.

With the **Progressive** power base that is influencing our present

Administration from the back room, they finally have a voice that can foster change.

The explosion of **Progressive** ideals on **America** reflects their new found influence and the need to accomplish a great deal in a short period of time. If they can change who we are before we realize that they are taking us down a path that we will never recover from, they might pull this off.

Unfortunately, we owe a great disservice to the once proud **Democratic Party** for failing to notice the growing power of the **Progressive Movement** within their ranks.

To be fair, both parties have a large number of followers that choose to vote along party lines, without doing the research as to what each candidate actually plans on doing when in office.

This time, however, the uninformed voter has done untold damage to our **Republic**.

In their desire to vote along party lines, no matter the issue or candidate, they successfully allowed a movement that does not reflect many of their core beliefs to run the country and alter our way of governing that has proven successful for centuries.

COMMON SENSE MOMENT - The Use of Racism as a weapon

The Progressives chose Racism as a means to an end because of its immediate impact on society. Calling anyone a racist has the affect of not continuing the dialogue but ending it.

If they can shut down conversation so easily using Race as a weapon, then charging our entire nation with Racism might have the same result.

The Progressives are well aware that the facts, along with the

independent nature of the American people, are not favorable to their cause.

They cannot sustain an intelligent dialogue on the values of Socialism and its merits when comparing it to Capitalism. They need to shut down the dialogue and amp up the emotion by using a topic that sends most people into hiding.

Once again, Racism fits the moment.

To say they have succeeded in winning a number of battles would be an understatement. Thanks to their partners in the Media and Big Tech, we are not having the much needed debate on the subject.

Through the unholy alliance that the Progressives have with the Media, their message is being broadcast to everyone in America without scrutiny or objective commentary. Just accept the fact that we are a Racist nation and lets just see where we go from there.

Its time to push back on that message and not let the masses believe it has any merit whatsoever. We are not a Racist nation and we should not let anyone tell us differently.

If we can take a step back and force an intelligent dialogue on Racism, the Progressives might not just lose a battle, they may lose the war.

Their message cannot succeed if we can place their true motives in front of average Americans. Allowing sunlight to expose them for what they are, could end this assault on our Republic before it takes hold of our nation and our freedoms.

Like a vampire who hides in the shadows, let's bring them out into the light of day and see if they can handle the exposure.

Two of the more egregious examples of the **Media** touting the **Progressive Agenda** and telling just the slanted, less truthful versions of the story, can be found in their bias reporting of the two most publicized and misunderstood issues of our day:

BLACK LIVES MATTER (BLM)
THE STATE OF LAW ENFORCEMENT

Both of these highly publicized issues are linked closely with **Racism** by the **Media** and the **Progressives.**

Observing them through the prism of **Racism** is necessary if the **Progressives** are going to use these issues to transform our society from one of personal responsibility and freedom into a society that depends on the collective for all of our needs.

Let's begin with **Black Lives Matter.** A movement that the **Progressives** desperately want to exploit for their own purposes.

BLACK LIVES MATTER

It is astonishing just how much traction the **BLM** movement has had on our society. They have taken an innocent slogan that just about every **American** can agree with and turned it into a cause that does not even resemble the inherent intent suggested by the slogan.

If every **American** did their own research on the organization known as **Black Lives Matter**, they would find a **Marxist** movement that is at odds with a few of the basic principles that help make us the country we are today.

1. **The Nuclear Family**

It's hard to oppose the value that the **Nuclear Family** has had on our society but that is exactly what the **BLM** movement is proclaiming.

One of the bedrocks of our society has always been the traditional family, consisting of a mother and father who raise their children as a family, with their influence shaping each child from birth to adulthood.

This does not mean that there are not other, less traditional family dynamics that can provide similar value to a child during the formative years of their life.

The value of the nuclear family is not restricted to parents that stay together while raising their children.

Divorced parents, who choose to raise their children together and with a stable bond that does not turn the children into pawns in their own personal disputes, can provide a positive and productive atmosphere for nurturing their children through their adolescence.

The growing number of same sex parents, who place the job of parenting above all else, can provide society with well adjusted and productive members of society that we are proud to welcome into the fold.

There are a number of studies over the years that suggests children who are missing the influence of one of their parents have a more difficult time adjusting and usually have less structure in their lives as they take the journey toward adulthood.

One of the reasons suggested by psychologists center on the fact that children who are raised without one of their parents, may develop problems along the way due to a lack of role models. That can lead to selecting someone for that role that is not part of their family unit.

Many of these exterior role models, especially in problem environments, can foster crime, drugs and other behavior that falls under the umbrella of anti-social behavior.

Inner-city crime among our minority communities has been the cause of death and tragedy for decades.

The overwhelming statistic that approximately **70%** of African American children are being raised in single parent households, most often without a father, has been one statistic that might explain the lack of hope and the lack of personal discipline that could lead many of these young minds to see no future for them beyond the streets.

When examining the statistical anomalies that the African American community experiences due to a disproportionate number of unwed mothers, we may be able to better understand why the **Black Lives Matter Movement** has chosen to dismiss the value of the **Nuclear Family**.

Rather than take on the task of trying to institute change among the black community that fosters the benefits of avoiding out of wedlock pregnancy, which is the primary cause of fatherless homes, they have chosen to discredit the value of the **Nuclear Family**.

The love and support of a solid family environment has always been at odds with the **Marxist** playbook. The only family that matters is the **State**. If the **State** cannot provide it, it has no importance.

One's loyalty and allegiance to one's family is considered a threat and needs to be broken, discarded or at the very least, minimized.

Why did the Nazi's use children to turn on their family and fellow citizens in support of the collective? When you break apart the family and pit them against each other, you have succeeded in removing resistance from the equation.

According to the **Black Lives Matter Movement**, nothing should stand in the way of elevating the **State** as the answer to all your needs, especially the **Nuclear Family**.

BLM proudly promotes a **Marxist** philosophy that fosters entitlements and reparations over individual accomplishments and initiative.

If they followed through with supporting all blacks, no matter their circumstance, it would be easier to accept them as representatives of their race rather than opportunists who seize on issues over substance.

2. The Destruction of Capitalism

Obviously, the **BLM** movement has chosen a path that few would have been surprised they would take to combat our **Capitalistic** Society, which is **Racism**.

Capitalism is **Racist** in their eyes and needs to be destroyed and discarded if our country is to pull itself out of our biased and unfair heritage, which is bent on subjugating our minority population, especially the **African American** community.

After all, **Capitalism** rewards the wealthy and advantaged with all of the opportunities necessary to succeed while the minority community wallows on the lower rungs of society with little chance of success.

Black and Brown citizens do not have any of the opportunities afforded white citizens in this country, or so they claim.

They are less educated because of the limited opportunities afforded them, and less capable of smashing through the many barriers that **Capitalism** places in their way.

These claims have little merit on face value. It's a far cry from isolated examples of prejudice and bias, which we know exists, to painting our entire system as being responsible for the misfortunes that minorities have had to endure over the years.

When you use a slogan that no **American** disagrees with and pretends that it justifies a movement that favors **Marxism** over **Capitalism**, you are trying to fool our citizens into blaming the system. That can lead to changing the system, which is the **Progressive's** plan all along.

The **Progressives** have succeeded in getting many large corporations to acquiesce to their demands and support an organization that has their ultimate destruction in mind.

How can such giants of industry as Bank of America, Coca Cola and Nike for example, possibly ignore the assaults coming from such a widely accepted slogan? It would be **Un-American** to do so, would it not?

Because of the pressure from the **Progressives,** including their most formidable weapon, **Cancel Culture**, Corporate **America** has donated hundreds of millions of dollars to an organization that has nothing to do with the slogan.

Under the fear of being canceled or marked as **racists**, these corporations have chosen to fund this bogus organization in the hope that they will, for lack of a better term, leave them alone when the assault on **Capitalism** begins in earnest.

The **Black Lives Matter** protests and riots across the country last summer that ended with billions of dollars in property damage and dozens of lives lost, are perfect examples of how we can lose our way and fail to see a movement for what it really is because their name is beyond reproach in a civilized society.

COMMON SENSE MOMENT - the BLM Movement

Can a cause be just if merely the mention of two similar slogans that deserve as much attention, are condemned and demeaned to such a degree by Blacks Lives Matter as to result in the loss of jobs and the loss of social standing by those foolish enough to proclaim their value to society?

Of course I'm taking about ALL LIVES MATTER and BLUE LIVES MATTER, two innocent and socially acceptable slogans that do nothing to diminish the value of BLM'S tagline.

Unfortunately, an organization that claims to be concerned about the lives of minorities in this country are not at all interested in accepting any slogan that does not compute with their agenda.

Maybe the answer lies in the fact that these Marxist supporters

are not really as concerned about Blacks Lives as they are with advancing the Progressive agenda of true Socialism at the expense of Capitalism.

I would think that an organization that truly believes in helping raise the Black minority status in this country and protecting them from all attacks, no matter the source, would be interested in combating Black on Black crime across the nation?

How come there are no marches and protests in Chicago, where Black youth are dying in record numbers in the streets at the hands of other Blacks?

How come the only crimes of importance to them involve white assailants, especially police officers, when a black life is lost, no matter the circumstance?

The real answer that must be shown the light of day is that they only care about the lives of minorities that can successfully further their political agenda of turning America into a Marxist utopia in which the STATE is the master of all that matters and every citizen's dependency on the STATE results in Equal outcomes, not opportunity.

That is not an America we should look forward to living in.

We have succeeded and thrived over the past two centuries by being a meritocracy that allows its citizens the opportunity to achieve based on their own abilities, desires and work ethic, not by being handed a stipend from the government.

Personal freedom is more than just one's ability to live free in a free society. It's the freedom to choose which path you will take in life that leads you to where you want to go.

Obtaining a good job and financial security requires a commitment that goes beyond the basics.

For those of us who have not inherited wealth, it is a path that

requires hard work, significant knowledge and a drive that refuses to allow roadblocks to get in our way.

While many minorities have often faced roadblocks over the years that were immovable, you cannot say that most of those are still in place today.

Personal bias and prejudice will be with us until the end of time but the laws have changed as have the attitudes and sentiments of the majority of Americans.

Its time to listen to your gut and trust your Common Sense gene. We are not a Racist nation that refuses to allow minorities a path to succeed. That's what the Progressives and their Black Lives Matter supporters would like you to believe.

Getting ahead and succeeding is beyond your control, if you are a minority, according to BLM. Our Racist country will not permit you to succeed, therefore your failures are inevitable and there's nothing you can do about it.

Based on that logic, why even try? Let the State provide you with the basics so that you can barely get by because that is all you're going to achieve anyway.

Capitalism is your enemy because they care little about your success. The STATE is your friend because it will provide for you regardless of your present status.

When an organization and a political ideology tries to convince you that you are a victim and will always remain a victim as long as Capitalism remains in the way, that to me is the definition of Racism, since they are telling you that you do not have the power to change your position in life nor the drive to do so.

When the Progressives are telling you to take these entitlement handouts because you are never going to succeed on your own, that is the most destructive message anyone could hear in America.

It should send a message to all of America that Racism comes in many forms, the most devastating being the absence of HOPE.

We need to pull back the curtain on the **Black Lives Matter Movement** and not allow ourselves to get caught up in the slogan.

BLM does not hide their **Marxist** preferences. They believe in the Progressive talking points in which minorities are entitled to **EQUITY** rather than **EQUALITY.**

They believe that outcomes are not a result of one's work ethic, educational standing or determination but an unfortunate by-product of their race.

When everyone has the same outcome, no one can alter their destiny because it's no longer under their control. That is true **Marxism** in a nutshell.

Did I fail to mention that under **Marxist** control, the ruling class will have unrivaled power and wealth and the class system will be in full swing? We will be a country of **HAVES** and **HAVE NOTS**, not a free society that permits merit to be rewarded.

That's not a country I care to live in.

CHAPTER SIX

Law and Order - Key to a Free Society

There are certain rights that every person expects from those in charge no matter where they call home.

At the top of that list is a system of **Law and Order** that permits citizens to remain safe to pursue their daily activities knowing that others in power are looking out for them and will react with force, if necessary, if their safety and well being is in jeopardy.

The need to disrupt the status quo, when it comes to **Law and Order,** is one of the tactics that the **Progressives** insist upon in order to weaken our resolve and leave the door ajar to change.

When the **Progressives** latched on to the **Black Lives Matter Movement** and saw an opportunity to weaken the credibility of our **Law Enforcement**, they jumped in with both feet.

Here was a chance to use **Race** as the tool that might damage our dependency on the police and weaken our resolve enough to convince the masses that police officers were not the beacons of service and protection we thought they were.

Once enough doubt is created regarding their motives, the **Progressives** can question the laws that are their to punish those that step out of line. That can lead to a total loss of credibility in the judicial system and open the door to alternatives that preach tolerance while creating chaos in the process

Law Enforcement - In the Crosshairs of the Progressives

We have approximately **800,000** Law Enforcement Officers in our country.

Every race, creed and gender are represented and, in some markets, such an inner city communities, minority representation in Law Enforcement reflect the majority of officers in those communities.

Obviously, the charge of **Systemic Racism,** a common theme coming out of the **Progressive** camp, does not extend to the hiring practices of our law enforcement agencies.

When you have such a large number of minority officers on the job, who are charged with protecting and serving our **330** million citizens, it seems to be a bit incredulous to suggest that the system is inherently **racist**.

The **racist** policies and practices that the **Progressives** would like us to believe are rampant throughout law enforcement, would require a level of cooperation among the officers whose job it is to implement those policies.

That would require many of our law enforcement officers to be **racists** themselves, no matter their ethnic background or skin color.

Common Sense should tell us that **Racist** policies would be difficult, if not impossible, for non racist officers who would be responsible for enforcing those policies, to accept and implement.

Be that as it may, let's look into some of the facts that the **Progressives** would prefer you do not see.

- For the fiscal year **2019,** a report published in the **Washington Post** of all places, indicated that the number of arrests in the country amounted to nearly **4** million, with the total number of deaths at the hands of the police being less than **1,100.**
- When you drill down further, you find that there were less than **50** occasions where the police killed **unarmed** suspects either by accident or out of necessity. Out of that number, there were only **9 African Americans** that lost their lives.
- Each and every case involving **African American** deaths were investigated thoroughly resulting in **three** officers being found guilty of negligence. All three were sent to jail for their actions.
- The remaining **6** cases involved aggressive actions on the part of the suspects who were being apprehended, including attempts to run down the officers with their cars or over-powering an officer during a scuffle that led to the need for another officer to take drastic measures.
- Out of **4** million arrests and over **1,000** altercations that resulted in the death of a suspect, less than **10** involved unarmed **African Americans**.

COMMON SENSE MOMENT

Based on those numbers, does your COMMON SENSE gene tell you that there is Systematic Racism in law enforcement?

No one is saying that there are not a number of bad cops on the force. Out of 800,000 there has to be number of bad apples that need to be shown the door or the inside of a cell.

No one doubts that a number of officers might be biased toward minorities and willing to harass or subject minorities to undue scrutiny when encountered during their shift.

I'm sure everyone looking to clean up the ranks would hope that, once these racist officers are exposed for their beliefs, they are prevented from harassing another citizen under the guise of enforcing the law.

However, this is a far cry from accusing our entire Law Enforcement community of being Systemically Racist.

The facts tell us otherwise and I'm sure that your Common Sense gene must be telling your gut the same thing. We are being lied to in order to advance an agenda that requires us to accept a claim that is indefensible.

The **Progressives** picked up the mantle of **Racism** in Law Enforcement after the events of **Ferguson Missouri** in which an unarmed black man was killed by a white officer.

While typical race baiters have been going after the police for years, the national attention this incident garnered gave the **Progressives** the perfect opportunity to exploit the issue to their advantage.

With the nation focused on this incident, a friend of **Mr. Brown**, who died at the hands of the police officer, decided to lie to the authorities in a way that started a movement across the country that still exists to this day.

He claimed that **Mr. Brown** put his hands in the air and proclaimed that he was giving up, pleading with the officer not to shoot him, seconds before the officer fired his weapon.

It was later proven that such an incident never happened. It was also proven that **Mr. Brown** was the aggressor and that the officer had no choice but to fire his weapon or be assaulted, possibly even killed, at the hands of a repeat offender that had no intention of standing down.

The **"Hands Up, Don't Shoot"** lie was used by those looking to take down law enforcement for months, well after the time that the true story was public knowledge.

Once again, it was the **Media** that fostered the lie by pretending that this was just another example of how **Law Enforcement** was inherently **Racist**.

The slogan even made its way on to the backs of **NBA** players for a brief period as the **NBA** permitted anti-racist slogans to replace player's names on their jerseys.

The entire country began to place blame on the police for all kinds of **racist** actions and there was no turning back for the **Progressives**. They had a catalyst to further drive our country apart on a sensitive issue and there was no way they were going to let it go.

When emotion, hatred and distrust can be fostered based on a lie, the results are still the same. The **Progressives** want us to believe that cops are killing blacks at a record pace and its time to do something about it.

This ongoing lie could easily be debunked by the main stream **Media** if they chose to do so but we already know the answer to that question.

The impact of painting all Law Enforcement with a broad brush of **Racism** has led to numerous deaths, the loss of billions of dollars in property damage and the defunding of police forces, either partially or substantially, all across the country.

These protests and false claims of **Racism** made it impossible for police officers to properly do their jobs and has weakened them significantly, during a time when the level of crime in our country requires the exact opposite in order to protect all of us.

The resulting riots in the summer of 2020 that the **Black Lives Matter Movement** encouraged, based on a lie, will remain a stain on our nation for decades to come.

The **Media's** failure to investigate the validity of these claims, choosing to accept the rants of a few radicals, has led to serious consequences.

Charges as serious as these require significant proof, though none were provided.

Instead we got every isolated instance of bad behavior on the part of law enforcement (**George Floyd** comes to mind) broadcasted loudly and continuously for all to see as the **Media** reinforced the claims of the **Progressives**, by trying to connect dots that are not there.

I observed a number of **"Man on the Street"** interviews that questioned average citizens who are not that into politics, which by the way represents the majority of **Americans**.

Most of us may watch our local news programs periodically and read a number of headlines on line but getting into the weeds of the political landscape is not on our radar.

I was shocked how many of these people thought the number of unarmed blacks killed by police were in the thousands. After all, a country as large as ours would expect nothing less based on the claims of **Racism** within the ranks.

What is insane is how the Main Stream **Media** refused to correct this misconception? When you repeat false claims as if they were fact, without questioning them, you are no longer acting as journalists.

There is more to **Fake News** than just misrepresenting the facts.

You do not have to lie to be a source for disinformation. When you job is to be the watchdog of truth, choosing to ignore that responsibility is the same as telling the public that these reports must be true.

COMMON SENSE MOMENT - The Law Enforcement Lie

While it is obvious that the race issue can be used to divide the country and create animosity, why the need to paint Law Enforcement as being public enemy #1?

The answer to that question requires a brief reminder of the goal of the Progressives.

If they are to achieve a breakdown of our core beliefs regarding how America functions, they need to not only divide us and pit us against each other, they need to establish distrust in our basic supportive networks, including our safety.

How better to do that than have us no longer believe that Law Enforcement is providing the protection that we so desperately need.

Making the police the enemy leads to the need for something else to take its place that will provide the necessary protections that we will require on a daily basis.

When your goal is to replace our form of government with another, you cannot allow any obstacles to get in the way, especially if those obstacles have guns and skills that could make things difficult for them during the transition.

Let's take a look at what all of the Socialist and Marxist regimes have done before they instituted their new order?

- *TAKE AWAY THE GUNS - Do not allow the people the means to defend themselves, including the local police departments. That's why all of this push for gun control, which really means gun confiscation. Whenever faced with a gun crime, the only words coming out of the mouths of the Progressives are how bad the guns are, not the criminals.*

- ***TAKE AWAY OUR FREEDOM TO SPEAK - Do not allow the people to exercise their rights under the 1st Amendment. Limit their expression to acceptable topics and opinions that reflect the views of the government or face censure and possible cancellation by their two accomplices, the Media and Big Tech.***
- ***TAKE AWAY OUR RIGHT TO CHOOSE - Do we get the vaccine or do we choose not to do so? Do we wear a mask or do we choose not to do so? These basic rights to choose are nowhere to be found in many of the states that have decided to join forces with the Progressives in power.***
- ***They claim its for our own good but that's exactly what EVERY Socialist or Marxist regime has said just before they took the right to choose away.***
- ***When the President and the Party in power mandate compliance, we have already gone too far in the process. We have lost the right to choose and we are closer to their objective of a society willing to comply rather than object.***

Law Enforcement is one of the many weapons we have to combat anarchy in this country. That's why it needs to be minimized in power and influence, according to the **Progressive** playbook.

The whole **DEFUND THE POLICE** movement is geared toward reducing the power and making it harder for the police to do their jobs.

If they are failing to keep us safe or they have lost the ability to judge everyone fairly and equally, then they no longer deserve the trust of the people.

Maybe its time to consider another form of protection, one that comes from the **Federal Government**. After all, they might do a better job and they are more inclusive and less prejudicial, or so they claim.

When you replace safety with fear, you open the door to change. The people will care less who is in charge as long as they feel safe in their homes.

One of the Architects of the Progressive Movement

Many of you have heard of **George Soros.** He's a billionaire that has made it his mission to upset the apple cart of law and order on the grass roots level. He is a staunch **Progressive** who has taken it upon himself to be their benefactor.

He is committed to disrupting many of the more influential local elections by investing in fellow **Progressive** candidates that could have the greatest influence on policy and procedures if elected to office.

He understands that many of the laws, and the necessary enforcement of those laws, are local in nature. Change local politics and you change our grass roots system of **Law Enforcement**.

He has made it his mission to get as many local **Progressive District Attorney's** into power as possible. With the aid of millions of dollars, that are far beyond the limited funds normally associated with these local races, he has succeeded beyond his expectations.

He realized a long time ago that the laws alone are not the answer. Getting them changed is difficult and time consuming and there are no guarantees of success.

Instead, he could have a lot more success by replacing the law makers in charge with someone willing to either ignore the laws in place or be willing to interpret their meaning beyond the original intent.

He has been spending millions of dollars on local elections to great success. Many of the larger cities now have **Progressive District Attorney's** that are ignoring the laws on the books and turning our system of justice into a social experiment.

Many of these **Progressive** District Attorney's believe that our system of justice is **Racist** by nature and in need of modification, regardless of the laws on the books.

If the law is too difficult to change, just ignore it and pretend that you are doing so for the good of the people.

Because of these **Racist** laws that are in place, according to the **Progressives**, many of those in prison are there unjustly and that needs to change.

Two ways to do that without changing the laws are **Bail Reform** and **Sentencing Reform**.

The results have been horrendous. Thousands of hardened criminals have been allowed back on the street as if **ALL** of them are innocent of their crimes, which is not even close to being factual.

COMMON SENSE MOMENT - The War at the Local Level

How has George Soros been able to have so much success?

Just take a moment to think about your own personal experiences when it comes to elections. We all are aware of the primary candidates in any election.

We know who is running for President, Senate and Congress at any given time and we, most likely, already know who we plan on pulling the lever for well before we go to the polls.

We are also aware that on every election ballot there are a number of other races going on that have less significance to a large majority of the voters but require our vote in order to gain office, from District Attorneys all the way down to School Board members.

While the primary candidates for the top offices are spending hundreds of thousands of dollars, possibly millions of dollars, on advertising in order to gain name recognition and influence voters

to their position on issues, the remaining candidates down ballot have very little money at their disposal.

The tactic used for the down ballot candidates rely mostly on an attempt to get name recognition and the hope that their party affiliation will garner support from voters who prefer voting along party lines.

George Soros understands this and he has chosen to throw a monkey wrench into the process by backing Progressive candidates with so much money that they become recognizable to the average voter on election day.

Just imagine how successful a Progressive candidate for District Attorney can be if they have **ONE MILLION DOLLARS** ***to spend on their campaign while their opponent is spending $100,000. Thousands of voters will remember their name when in the booth while their opponent might be unrecognizable.***

When it comes to Democratic controlled municipalities, where the outcome is less in doubt, Soros will spend the majority of his funds during the primaries to make sure that his candidate wins the race, eliminating any moderate Democrat from obtaining office.

By outspending their less Progressive challengers in their own party in the primaries, Soros uses the higher name recognition that he has bought and paid for to secure the nomination for his radical candidate, guaranteeing the Progressives their seat at the table come election day.

I, for one, have decided to avoid supporting anyone on my ballot that I know little about. I've learned a long time ago that voting just because they are affiliated with my party of choice, is a bad mistake.

While I try to research more than just the major candidates, most of the names below those candidates remain a mystery to me and therefore, will have to get their votes from others.

Racism and the Law

As stated earlier, thanks to the efforts of **George Soros**, the **Progressives** in power are using their control of law enforcement to spread greater division among the citizens by pretending that the Laws in place are fostering **Racism**.

They would like us to believe that our present laws are **racist** and need to be ignored if we are to achieve **Social Justice.**

Social Justice is a catch phrase that provides the necessary justification to bend the law to conform to their warped interpretation of it's meaning in order to achieve the desired effect in the field.

George Soros's success in placing extreme **Progressives** into **District Attorney** positions in dozens of cities across the country, especially in some of our major cities, has resulted in a rise in crime of untold proportions.

He has managed to secure DA'S in New York, Chicago, Los Angeles, San Francisco, Philadelphia, Austin, Portland and Seattle, to name a few, who are creating a divide that has led to a crime wave that rivals anything our country had seen since the turbulent sixties.

How are these policies related to **Racism**?

If the **Progressives** believe that our entire Law Enforcement community is **Systemically Racist**, then the support systems must be **racist** as well, which includes the **Penal System**.

Now we get to the center of the issue that ties **Racism** to **Crime**. While the black and brown population in **America** remain in the minority, they are responsible for a majority of the crimes committed every year.

This is a statistical fact that cannot be ignored or disputed.

There are many reasons why this might be happening, including the high number of crimes being committed in the inner cities, which happens to be predominantly home to black and brown minorities.

Throw in the high volume of drug offenses, which lead to crime, controlled by inner city gangs who are predominantly minorities, and you can see how the high number of criminals in the system could favor a particular race, even though they make up a minority of the overall population.

Along comes our **Progressive** elites that are looking to enforce their skewed view of **Social Justice** and we have another war to fight that can only further widen the divide.

They are using emotion rather than fact to tell us just how unfair our system can be to those minorities without the necessary resources to defend themselves.

Rather than looking at the actual crime statistics, they choose to tell us that the only reason the prison system is housing a majority of minorities behind bars has to do with our **racist** tendencies that has led to these unfortunate individuals being falsely incarcerated because of the color of their skin by a **racis**t system that exists under the guise of **Law Enforcement.**

I have no doubt that there are a number of people in jail that should not be there. In a country this large and a system of justice that is all encompassing, there are going to be times where either the wrong man or woman gets convicted of a crime or faces a more severe punishment than they might deserve.

That's a far cry from the **Progressive's** claim that our entire **Justice System** is corrupt along **racist** lines and needs to be reimagined (a popular word among the **Progressive** elite).

When these agenda driven **District Attorneys,** who owe their job to

George Soros, along with a number of well placed **Progressive Court Judges**, try to convince us how broken our **Penal System** is, they fail to remind us how most of the people we have placed behind bars really need to be there.

The reasons behind the creation of our **Penal System** can be summed up with an understanding of the two "P"s that make up the entire purpose behind its existence:

- **Punishment**
- **Protection**

While the **Progressives** would like us to believe that the entire system is based on **punishment**, they ignore the other half of the equation.

Besides **punishing** those that break our laws, we need to **protect** our law abiding citizens from having to interact with known criminals that have little regard for our possessions or our personal safety.

When criminals interact with regular citizens, it always ends badly, sometimes deadly, for the innocent citizen.

Our jails are more than **punishment**, they are **protection** from the worst that our society has to offer.

When you allow these **District Attorney's** to empty the jails in the name of **Racial Justice**, you are ignoring the need to protect us from those willing to do us harm.

It is a known fact that career criminals will not change their ways once they leave the Penal System. The rate of recidivism is huge among these law breakers and the vast majority of them go on to commit more crimes and injure more of our citizens without any remorse or reflection.

When these **Progressives** release known criminals by pretending that they are only there because of a racist system of Law and Order, they bring more crime and death in their wake, leaving us less safe and more afraid to lead our lives as we wish to do.

The results of these **WOKE** policies have been dramatic.

We now have higher crimes statistics in all categories as an obscene number of career criminals, put back on the streets by these radical **District Attorneys**, feel emboldened by the fact that they have been given a green light to continue their unlawful ways with impunity.

Add in a demoralized **Law Enforcement** community that has their hands tied behind their backs and you have a perfect storm of corruption and inaction that can only lead to more crime and more loss of life.

Recently, a young Asian model was waiting in a New York City subway station and was grabbed from behind and assaulted on the subway platform. She was beaten and groped by the assailant before he stole her pocketbook and left her bleeding on the concrete platform.

When the perpetrator was apprehended, we learned that he had a total of **44** arrests over a twenty year period, including some serious crimes of assault and battery.

He was identified three months prior as the perpetrator in a robbery that resulted in the store clerk being pistol whipped before he exited the store.

It took the justice system three months to issue an arrest warrant, permitting him to remain free to attack that woman in the subway.

Tell me how the local **District Attorney**, along with the J**udge** hearing the case, could possibly think that this person was worthy of being put back on the streets?

How do you think the police officers, who collared this person numerous times over the past two decades, feel to find him back on the streets committing crime after crime?

We are going down a path that is extremely dangerous. Under the guise that these criminals are actually victims of a **racist** system of justice can only lead to more crime and more death.

Every minority arrested and placed in the system is not an innocent person who tried drugs for the first time or stole a loaf of bread to feed their family. You cannot run a safe and orderly city by turning the facts upside down to fit your narrative.

Trying to protect that one person out of a hundred that was unfairly treated by the system, by pretending that ninety-nine out of a hundred are the real victims of that system, ignore the needs of the innocents. Our system of justice needs to protect us from those that wish to do us harm.

When you fail to enforce the **Punishment,** you fail to provide the **Protection** that you vowed to do when you took the oath of office.

Every civil servant from the **President** on down vows to **Serve and Protect**. Everyone that ignores their basic promise needs to be voted out of office or removed from their duties.

In the meantime, every **American** citizen is less safe and secure today thanks to the release of hardened criminals on to our streets by **Progressive District Attorney**s and **Judges t**hat view their responsibilities through rose colored glasses.

We owe much of the rise in crime and our unsafe streets, with known criminals roaming free, to the efforts and the money of **George Soros**.

The Importance of Law and Order

In a country where just about everything has a political element, the one bastion of sanity and control used to be our system of **Law and Order**. Politics had no role in our judicial system. If you commit the crime, you should do the time.

All of the laws on our books were developed over centuries to protect our freedoms and our citizens from lawlessness and chaos, the two things that could jeopardize our safety and our sense of security.

The **Scales of Justice Symbol** wears a blindfold for a reason. No matter the race, creed, gender or political persuasion of anyone in the courtroom, the promise of fair and equitable treatment, under the law, is expected and demanded.

If we can no longer count on the justice system to protect our rights and freedoms from attack, we can no longer be a society that possesses the necessary **Checks and Balances** that the majority of average citizens who follow the law have come to expect.

In fact, in my opinion, **Law and Order** are the key elements that make **America** so desirable to the rest of the planet.

We might expect our political leaders to profit from their position of leadership and to benefit from their position of power, as the polls might suggest. I'm sure its one of the primary reasons that Congress has such a low favorability score.

However, when push comes to shove, our system of justice should never allow us to fall into anarchy, or so we thought.

When the **Progressives** challenged those beliefs by bending our laws in order to place their ideology above all else, they eroded the one system we counted on to keep politics and opinions at bay.

They could not have done more to weaken our resolve and threaten our security.

This may be the most dangerous part of their plan for reimagining **America**.

We need to find a way to expose their false claims of **Social Injustice** before they succeed in destroying our most basic defense against **Anarchy;** our system of **Law and Order.**

Common Sense Moment - The Real Danger

If the assault on Law and Order by the Progressives were limited to local interference and state controlled bureaucrats, it would still be serious and consequential, but correctable on election day.

If that were the case, many of those bureaucrats could be just one election away from losing their power entirely since all elected officials owe their positions of power to the voters who put them in office.

Unfortunately, it appears to be more problematic than just local officials who have lost their way.

There are DEEP concerns about the unelected officials that are in charge of our Federal branches of Law Enforcement.

When you have Progressive Agents embedded in both the Justice Department and the Federal Bureau of Investigation that are far more powerful than any local representative, you can ruin the country from within before our very eyes and there is little anyone can do about it.

My use of the term DEEP when discussing Federal bureaucrats is not an accident. The DEEP State is real and has power beyond the control of most of our elective officials.

Having a number of powerful non-elected bureaucrats in our judicial branch of government, acting in concert with the Progressive Administration, makes for a formidable foe that can withstand just about any attack from the opposition.

The following are examples of how our Federal Law Enforcement Agencies have chosen ideology over the law:

- *What does your Common Sense gene tell you when we have hundreds of citizens in jail right now for more than a year without being charged properly for their perceived crimes with no court date in sight?*

- *How is it that our Federal agents claim that these people are Insurrectionists who attempted to take down our government last January but have yet to be charged with anything, for the most part, beyond a charge of trespassing?*
- *Our Federal Justice system, under pressure from the Progressive left, have succumbed to that pressure and chose to strip all of these people of their rights as citizens, keeping them from their families without charging them with any crime serious enough to warrant such treatment.*
- *Don't you think that after one year and thousands of hours of video of the protest at the Capitol, they would have found enough evidence to charge them properly by now?*
- *I contend that if they had the evidence to do so, they would have charged them long ago. Instead, because the Progressives need for the country to believe that an insurrection occurred that fateful day, they have decided to punish these trespassers as if they committed treason based on nothing but their own desire to justify the claim of Insurrection where none exists.*
- *Our justice system needs to be non-political but they appear to be anything but neutral. You can't ignore the law and declare anyone guilty without proper evidence and an impartial day in court to defend themselves properly.*
- *The summer riots of 2020 had serious actions taken by rioters that resulted in billions of dollars in damages and hours of video tape showcasing actual criminals burning down buildings and assaulted officers with little or no jail time as a result.*
- *When you have politically charged Federal agencies that choose what laws to enforce and what laws to ignore, the*

freedoms guaranteed by our Constitution are no longer there to protect us. That's what happens in countries run by Despots who decide the actions that need be taken regardless of the laws on the books. Is that where America is heading?

- *What does your Common Sense gene tell you when the Attorney General of the United States, the top law enforcement officer in the country, agrees to accept advice from a national Teacher's Union and declare parents who protest at School Boards to be possible domestic terrorists?*
- *When you understand that their protests centered on government overreach stemming from mask mandates and the teaching of Critical Race Theory to their children, two Progressive sponsored activities, you must conclude that the Attorney General was doing the bidding of the politicians in charge, the last thing we need to see from those overseeing our law enforcement agencies.*
- *What does your Common Sense gene tell you when the FBI, who were in possession of Hunter Biden's laptop for more than a year, with no indication of any action whatsoever, fails to address the claims of financial abuse and the possibility of influence peddling that is clearly documented on the laptop?*
- *Could they still be deciding what to do in terms of legal action? Could they still be trying to validate the information? Could they be dragging their heels in hope that the issue will go away so that they did not have to act at all?*
- *The laptop has been validated as real. The problematic information on the laptop has been published and discussed by reputable journalistic sources and still the FBI refuses to address the issue.*

- ***If the FBI decides to dispute the charges of influence peddling, please do so and show us how you came to that conclusion. If the FBI needs more time to verify the content, please let us know.***
- ***Deciding to do nothing with such a volatile and public issue can only lead others to suspect that it would not bode well for the people in power to have official verification of what everyone already knows to be the truth.***
- ***For the FBI to choose politics over the law is one of the most dangerous things possible. We will never survive as a Republic if the law can be manipulated in such a way as to suggest that laws are made to be broken and one's political leanings can dictate which laws will be enforced and which will be ignored.***

We are in dangerous territory when we cannot trust our **Federal Law Enforcement Agencies** with enforcing the laws as written, not as one would prefer them to be.

If we allow politicians to have power over the **Law**, we will truly become powerless because our **Republic** will have become a dictatorship and none of us will be safe from their reach if we choose a different path to follow.

One of our **Founding Fathers, James Madison**, was well aware of what can happen when political power replaces the power of the people when he said:

"In Europe, charters of liberty have been granted by power. But America has set the example of charters of power granted by liberty. This revolution in the practice of the world may, with an honest praise, be pronounced the most triumphant epoch in history."

CHAPTER SEVEN

An Overview of Racism in America

It should be obvious to everyone that the use of **Racism** as a weapon for change is nothing new. **Americans** are well aware of their history and no one is proud of a time in our past where everyone could not benefit equally from what **America** had to offer.

I have always been told that before one can change their ways or their beliefs, they first must recognize their faults. Countries are not any different.

America recognized their inadequacies concerning **Race** nearly two centuries ago and fought a war to force compliance to the basic principle written in our Constitution: "**All Men are Created Equal**".

Because of this stain in our past history, every **American** remains constantly aware that **Racism** represents the worse of our societal history and we need to be ever vigilant in order to keep the sins of the past from gaining a foothold in the present.

The **Progressives** know this as well and have chosen to resurrect those fears and concerns in every **American** and use them against us to foster a change in **America** that can only happen through division and distrust among the masses.

Racism is a tool to be used by them to get us to comply to their demands. We need to see them for what they are and not for what they pretend to be.

We are not the same country that fought a **Civil War** for racial freedom. We are not the same country that fought for **Civil Rights** in the early sixties. We cannot let anyone, especially the **Progressives** looking to turn us into a **Socialist Natio**n, tell us otherwise.

The 1619 Project

In an effort to change our country into a **Socialist** nation that no longer values personal freedoms, individual accomplishments or one's ability to choose their own path, the **Progressives** have tied their wagon to a historically inaccurate account of **America**.

The **1619 Project**, written by Nikole Hannah-Jones, is an attempt to place the philosophical beginning of our nation some **160** years earlier than the **Declaration of Independence** and the **Constitution.**

According to Ms. Jones, while we may have changed from a colony under the rule of **Great Britain** to an independent nation in **1776**, who we are as a nation and what rules our consciousness, as well as our subconsciousness, has more to do with **1619** than it does with **1776**.

It was in **1619** that the first slave ships landed in the new world and that event forever changed who we are as a nation, according to Ms. Jones.

It appears that having raised generations upon generations with slavery in our past, we can no longer expect any **American** to be born that does not have the sin of slavery deeply embedded into their psyche.

The belief that the white race is racially superior to people of color cannot be wiped from our memories or our personal prejudices, thus we remain a **racist** nation, according to Ms. Jones.

These opinions expressed by Ms. Jones, and I emphasize that they are opinions, have been absorbed in its entirety by the **Progressive** movement and is the central argument for their theory that **America**, at its core, is a **Racist** nation and will remain one regardless of our efforts to change.

The **Progressives** would like us to believe that our true racist nature will eventually show itself and dictate our actions so that we will continue to place obstacles in the path of minorities, preventing them from achieving their full potential.

There is a lot of history that needs to be ignored if we are to believe the **1619** P**roject** and its **racial** conclusions.

Starting with the fact that most of the world engaged in the practice of **slavery** at the time we were following that same path. **Slavery** is far from an **American** sin against humanity.

She failed to note that the practice of **slavery** continued in many countries long after **America** decided to break from the practice, including the need for us to fight a bloody **Civil War** to force those who resisted the concept of **Freedom for All** into compliance**.**

If Ms. Jones is correct about her underlying premise that we have little control of our inherent **racist** tendencies and are incapable of being unbiased, consciously or unconsciously, it would suggest that minorities are never going to be permitted to excel anywhere on the planet, not just in the good old **USA**, since the world is as guilty of the sin of **Racism** as is **America.**

When you believe that the world is systemically **racist** and minorities are just going to have to live with the fact that they are going to remain suppressed until eternity, you close all doors to change and create a sense of defeatism in our minority population that has no answers.

This is a dire look at society. The only path left to take is one that requires revolution instead of dialogue, resistance instead of compromise and government dependency instead of personal responsibility.

While it may be easy to brush this off as being utter nonsense, it takes on a much darker tone when our political leaders, including the head guy himself, are willing to spew this nonsense from the bully pulpit by agreeing with the premise that **America** is a **Systemically Racist** nation.

When you brand your nation as being **Systemically Racist**, how do you go on from there?

How do you then ignore your own remarks and continue to lead such a damaged and flawed nation that is beyond redemption as Ms. Jones suggests?

Maybe the Administration really did not understand the meaning of those remarks.

Maybe, in an attempt to garner the necessary support from the minority population to win an election, they failed to grasp the danger they authenticated by making those remarks.

Either way, its hard to ignore the implications and just carry on.

COMMON SENSE MOMENT - a Racist Nation

How did we ever get to this point?

How could we have gone from a nation that believes in Freedom and the rights of the individual to one of prejudicial policies and racist undertones that are tearing our nation apart from the inside out?

It is time to believe our own COMMON SENSE gene and ask ourselves if there is any truth to any of this nonsense.

I, for one, have no doubt that America is well beyond the early history of our nation and we are only going to head backwards if we allow such race baiters to continue to paint us with the brush of bigotry.

If what Ms. Jones claims had any truth, I doubt our nation would have ever survived and prospered as we have done for centuries.

The Declaration of Independence, the Constitution, the Terrible Civil War, the Civil Rights Movement of the Sixties, none of these forward progress events would have ever seen the light of day.

We are being played for fools and, thanks to the Progressive movement and their unrestricted access to our political leaders, we are being led down a path that can only lead to erasing the tremendous gains we have achieved by sending us back in time to an era where we were less tolerant of others, a time we thought long gone.

There is no better weapon for the **Progressives** to use on us than the stain of **Racism**. Every **American** is aware of our history and just the mention of bigotry can leave us in a place of insecurity.

For years, the best way to end a discussion was to call one's opponent a **Racist**.

The **Progressives** hope that calling the entire nation **Racist** will have the same result and allow then to continue their war on our way of life and keep the populous silent as they transform **America** into a place few of us would recognize.

Inclusiveness versus Segregation

Our nation has worked tirelessly for decades to eliminate all manners of **segregation**.

If we are to prosper, as our **Founding Fathers** envisioned, as **ONE NATION UNDER GOD**, then we must treat every **American** as an equal with the same rights and opportunities.

No one will ever claim that we are perfect or that any nation, for that matter, has or will ever reach perfection. The best we can hope for is to be aware of our frailties and to strive to correct them when they attempt to stop our progress toward inclusion.

The **Civil Rights** leaders of the past, including the most influential and most recognizable leader, **Martin Luther King**, fought the battle for equal rights and inclusion, not special considerations and special treatments.

He wanted us to stop seeing color and judge all **Americans** by their character, believing that only a color blind society can reach the goal of true equality for all.

When the **Progressives** decided that they needed to use **Race** as a wedge to further divide our country and pit citizen against citizen, they hoped that by creating a modern racial war, all **Americans** would be distracted enough to allow them to transform **America** in a way that would make it unrecognizable, before we had the chance to see it coming.

In other words, **Race** is a distraction, not the cause they pretend it is.

When you have to depend on emotion rather than fact, the **Progressives** understand that emotion can be a powerful weapon in the right hands. **Racial** tension can easily stir up sensitivities from the past and blind us to the facts.

The **1619 Project**, along with their insidious cousin, **Critical Race Theory**, is the perfect tools to stir hatred and division among decent people that thought we had evolved well beyond those frailties.

COMMON SENSE MOMENT - Racial Division

It's interesting to see that the Progressive's desire to send us back in time regarding racial issues to the era of Segregation and Inequality, is having an unexpected result that few anticipated.

It is my opinion that sooner or later, Americans will realize that all these claims of Racism will be harder and harder to justify.

When that point is reached, the alarm will go off and the country will wake up to the deception that the Progressives are attempting to use as a wedge to turn Americans against each other.

I believe the Progressives know this as well. Their plan is to change America BEFORE its citizens awaken to the deception that cleared the path to Socialism.

When you use a misguided tool, such as the 1619 Project, where the claim of embedded Racism leaves no room for improvement or redemption, you are left with a big problem.

If we are a nation that has grown with Racism being part of our very soul, as they suggest, there is nowhere for us to go that will correct this wrong except the path toward Division.

The Progressives backed themselves into a corner with the 1619 Project and the only path forward is to accept Segregation, Equity (a form of Reparations) and an impenetrable wall that separates all Americans by the color of their skin.

If you cannot succeed on your own, which is what they claim, then you need to exist on handouts and governmental support that bridges the gap between personal responsibility and personal achievement.

In other words, you need to depend on others rather than yourself. That's the perfect scenario for a Socialist nation that claims to

provide equally for its citizens while impeding and discouraging individual accomplishments and initiative.

An Unexpected Conundrum

During the times in our history when **Racism** was prevalent and out in the open, the unequal treatments being afforded to black minorities in our country were obvious to anyone willing to see the ugly truths that were right in front of their eyes.

The primary tool, at the time, in the **Racist's** handbook was **Segregation**.

In order to prevent even the possibility of equal treatment and opportunity for the oppressed, it was necessary to separate the black community from the rest of society by maintaining an atmosphere that suggests that our country was divided into two distinct societal camps; **US vs. THEM.**

What we were left with was a senses of confusion that left many average **Americans** with a sense of mystique about the black population.

Because of segregation, few white citizens ever interacted with the black community and that created a sort of mystique about them and their culture and traditions.

They could not drink out of the same water fountains. They were not permitted to sit at the same luncheonette counters or ride the same buses, sleep in the same motels or attend the same churches.

The act of **Segregation** was the greatest sin of all and left many **Americans** with an uncomfortable feeling about interacting with blacks on any level.

Today, all of that **Segregation** nonsense is behind us and we interact constantly, including a great deal of assimilation.

Interracial marriages and interactions are as common today as breathing. We share the same spaces and no one gives it a second thought nor should we.

Now here's the **Conundrum** that no one expected.

As the **Progressives** are trying to divide our nation along racial lines once again, it's the **Black** community, who have succumbed to this deception in greater numbers.

As they begin to suspect the **White** community of having **racist** tendencies, they are beginning to look toward **Segregation** as a tool to separate themselves from the rest of the population.

We are finding a number of **SAFE SPACES** at our Universities for the minority students to congregate among their own without interference from the white student body.

Many of our Colleges and Universities are offering separate graduation ceremonies that allow the minorities to receive their diplomas or degrees without the rest of the student body being present.

In an effort to stand out from the rest of society, they are using **Segregation**, the mortal sin of the **Racist Era**, to avoid having to interact with those that they deem to be **Racist.**

How did the desire among those that were experiencing prejudice decades ago change from the need to be accepted and included to the need to be separate?

Time to Express an Opinion

I have a definite opinion on this issue and this might be the right time for me to let you in on that opinion.

While my desire is to present facts in place of opinions, there are times when we have no facts at our disposal and the threat of allowing an issue to fester and grow is too great not to offer an opinion on the matter, so here it goes.

When looking back on our history, the signs of **Racism** were staring us in the face, not hidden behind curtains of deception.

During S**lavery,** no one needed to tell you that a particular race of people were being subjugated and treated less as fellow human beings and more like pieces of property.

When **Slavery** first ended in the **North** and eventually across the entire nation, the signs of continued subjugation were everywhere.

Not having the right to vote, the availability of proper educational opportunities, the failure to permit blacks access to all facets of society, were exposed for all to see. Those that chose not to look were as guilty as those who chose to enforce these unfair edicts.

Prior to the **Civil Rights Movement**, that gave birth to **Dr. Martin Luther King**, many of the sins of **segregation** were still out in the open, especially in the **South**.

In other words, we knew who the enemy was and we knew what needed to be done to combat the racially exclusionary part of our society that resisted change and failed to follow the words of the **Constitution**.

Since the tumultuous sixties, we have continued to progress beyond the obvious and while no one doubts that some form of **racism** will be with us until the end of time, **America** has done all the right things required to implement the changes that we once thought impossible to achieve.

Today, there is **NO** law that I'm aware of in any State or Federal Statute that permits **Racism** to legally exist in **America**. In other words, the law prohibits any and all expressions of **Bias** and **Racism** from taking place.

All outward expressions of **Bias,** such as **Segregation**, unfair labor practices, denial of educational opportunities, limiting access to employment or housing based on race, etc., are strictly prohibited.

What we are left with is impossible to quantify, which is the underlying prejudice of individuals and their impact on minorities, which is the core premise of the **1619 Project**.

So, if we are to believe that minorities are being persecuted because of the color of their skin and being denied the opportunities that whites enjoy, we have no tangible proof to point to in society.

When we have no laws that foster such **bias** and we have specific laws that punish anyone who chooses to act, in a tangible way, on expressing acts of **bias**, who do we blame for the inequities?

The **Progressives**, with their support network of race baiters, including the **1619 Project,** their punishment arm known as **Cancel Culture**, the **Media** and **Big Tech**, have had success in convincing many minorities that they are still being oppressed by society and need to make their voices heard once again, just like their ancestors had to do decades earlier.

The difference lies in identifying the enemy.

Is it our **Federal Government**? If so, how so? Is it **Corporate America**? How are they keeping minorities from gainful employment? Is it our educational system? How are minorities being denied access to equal education under the law?

When the answers are hard to define, the belief that the persecution still exists requires those suppressed to create an enemy and act upon it accordingly.

When the facts are not easily identified, its time to act on emotion, which fits well with the **Progressive Movement** that uses emotion over fact for just about everything.

The lack of tangible enemies among the minority population that has bought into the suppressed narrative has led to them willing to **segregate** from the rest of society in order to protect themselves from attacks and innuendoes that they have yet to identify but believe exists.

When you ignore the facts, you fail to see the irony that your emotions have exposed to society.

By choosing **segregation** over inclusion, you are turning the **Civil Rights Movement** on its head and creating the opposite of what past leaders hoped to achieve.

When you already have inclusion and equality under the law, the only path open to you is choosing to separate yourself from your imagined enemy and that leads to **Segregation**.

By creating a false narrative of **Racism** being inherently a part of society, the **Progressives** have begun to divide **America** along racial lines once again but this time, it's the oppressed who favor **Segregation** not the **Oppressors**.

We cannot allow the **Progressives** to divide us any further. If there are acts of prejudice being carried out by the **Racists** among us, then we need to expose those acts and denounce their implementation.

Shining a light on them and allowing the rest of us to see what used to exist behind the curtain is the only way to prevent **bias** from having a place in our society.

It is not enough for us to imply prejudice or pretend that it exist in the souls of the **American** people.

A world that allows prejudice to fester and grow based on inference and innuendoes is a world that is willing to permit emotion and fear to rule the day.

We are not a **racist** nation by any stretch of the imagination. We are not a country that sees **bias** behind every corner and looks to suppress an entire race because we have an inferior opinion of certain people because of the color of their skin.

If we let the **Progressives** tell us otherwise, we will be guilty of a much more dangerous sin; the sin of silence.

They are poisoning our society with their lies and are turning

Americans against each other for reasons that have nothing to do with race. Silence is no longer a path worth taking. We need to show them that we have a voice and that we are not afraid to use it.

Now that the **Progressive**s have hijacked the **Democratic Party** and have gained power, deciding to ignore them in hopes that they will just go away, no longer works. They will only assume that our silence suggests compliance, which is the opposite of what we need the world to know.

CHAPTER EIGHT

Indoctrination in our Educational System

The **Progressive** assault on our educational system precedes the existence of every **WOKE** member of the **Administration** and **Congress** by decades.

The **Progressives** have managed to infiltrate most of our **Colleges** and **Universities** with fellow believers that have been quietly indoctrinating our young adults with the principles of **Socialism**.

Because they have been at this for a long time, they have been able to replace many of the more traditional professors with **Progressives.**

As their reach extends into the many teaching colleges across the country, where the future educators of our youth will learn their trade, you can understand how extensive their influence has grown.

As the minds of our youth are in the developmental stages, they are open to influence beyond that of our more experienced adults, who have lived lives that include numerous instances of real world interactions rather than a world of rhetorical abstracts.

When you can spew all types of intellectual garbage without having to apply it to any tangible act, it can become attractive to an inexperienced mind and foster a sense of purpose that the young mind fails to see as a house of cards, ready to fall, with no foundation.

If the **Progressives** are to reimagine **America** in the image of

Socialism and **Marxism,** they need to begin with the youth who lack the necessary intellectual experience to question the veracity of their teachings.

One need not look further than a famous quote of **Lenin's** that explains the need to indoctrinate the young:

"Give me just one generation of youth and I'll transform the whole world"

Unfortunately, we may have allowed the **Progressives** to have more than one generation to work on and we are beginning to see the damage that has been done.

Critical Race Theory

While the **Progressives** have tied their wagon to the **1619 Project** in order to begin the process of turning **Americans** against one another along racial lines, they have adopted **Critical Race Theory** as the tool that will cement their hold on our youth for decades to come.

They no longer limit their efforts exclusively in the **Colleges** and **Universities**.

They have been able to indoctrinate a significant number of new teachers, at all grade levels, who are spreading their ideology among our most vulnerable in grades as low as kindergarten.

The process gets a lot easier if they can convert those that have yet begun the process of finding their own path. After all, our children are just beginning to think for themselves.

Understanding the benefits of beginning the indoctrination process earlier in the educational process are obvious. By the time they reach higher education, they have already been exposed and indoctrinated with **Socialist** and **Marxist** principles requiring less effort to turn them.

Therefore, we cannot make the mistake of concentrating all of our efforts on higher education. We must begin the process of rooting out these ideological indoctrination efforts earlier than originally thought.

What is Critical Race Theory?

You will not find it as a course in our schools. You will not find it listed as a definitive belief that has a name and a structure that needs to be studied and understood.

The last thing the **Progressives** want to do is shine a light on it so bright that it raises red flags, which can cause strong reactions among the adults, who might see it for what it is, a form of racial indoctrination.

Critical Race Theory takes the concepts reflected in the **1619 Project** and sets about adapting them to everyday life.

If every white **American** has **racial bias** in their **DNA**, then that suggests that all whites are not only inherently **racist** but have been living their lives with advantages and privileges that can only be described as **WHITE PRIVILEGE**, a state that needs to be corrected if we are to go forward as an all inclusive nation.

Critical Race Theory tells all white students that they, along with all of their ancestors, are privileged and have always been **racist** at their core.

More importantly, **Critical Race Theory** suggests that all whites are inherently the oppressors while all minorities, especially black **Americans,** are inherently the oppressed.

In order to obtain equal status for minorities, we have to create a country that does not depend on individual accomplishments and initiative, which they claim are already **biased**.

True equality will be achieved in our country when we accept **Socialism** rather than **Capitalism**. Only then can we achieve a more inclusive path in which the **State** provides for everyone's needs equally and without prejudice.

What needs to happen is for all whites to recognize their superiority and the **racial** undertones that fostered that superiority and begin to pay for their past sins by acknowledging its existence and accepting the consequences that those past sins have had on our society.

The first step is to identify their privileged heritage and apologize for it by altering future actions to reflect their new found **WOKE** understanding of how and why they were so blessed in **America.**

Only by recognizing the terrible affects their **racial bias** has had on the minority population can we move forward as a nation.

If you begin to believe any of this nonsense as having credence, you open the door to change and that door might never be closed.

As we have said on numerous occasions, language matters and it can hide the truth in plain sight more often than we care to recognize.

A lot of what they say and how they say it has been fine tuned for years so that the message can be sent disguised as something that no one can object to if they want to remain acceptable to the main stream.

If the **Progressives** can accomplish any of this, especially with unchallenged approval from average **Americans**, we might be well on our way to a **Socialist** nation.

The Unexpected Gift

The recent pandemic has created numerous problems that are still being addressed more than two years after the first outbreak.

Shutting down our entire economy was unprecedented and remains problematic on a number of fronts to this day, especially among our school children and how they are being forced to deal with changes that appear to have long term consequences, primarily with their social development.

Children learn a great deal while in school that has nothing to do with their academic classes.

As a child breaks away from the home environment and begins interacting with other children without their parents being close by, they begin to form the necessary social skills that will serve them well for the rest of their lives.

Thanks to the pandemic, children first had to deal with trying to learn remotely with no direct interaction with anything but a computer screen.

When given the opportunity to attend classes at school, they were forced to wear uncomfortable masks for hours a day without seeing the faces of their teachers or other children, a key element of emotional growth.

Whether these strict, protective measures were necessary is a discussion for another day, but parents learned a great deal more than they expected because of the need to re-imagine the classroom.

When school boards decided that it was too dangerous for our children to interact with their teachers and fellow students in the classroom, the need for another form of education was required or our children would be left behind even further.

The solution was zoom classes that could be conducted at home on the computer screen for every child that had access to a computer.

The teacher would conduct their lessons via the screen and the hope was that every child's educational needs would continue as planned, just from a different type of classroom.

For the first time, parents were able to see what their children were being taught.

What the teachers and the **Progressives** failed to realize was that parents, in many cases, were attending their classes from afar, a pleasant change from having to ask their children the universal questions about school and their daily interactions.

How was your day? What did you learn today? These are universal questions that have been staples in our society for decades. Most parents know that they rarely got any information of substance in return.

The usual response of **NOTHING** or a general response that suggested their day was **OKAY**, were common responses that told the parents nothing of substance.

By observing the actual classroom interaction, the parents began to notice that there was a lot more being discussed besides **Reading, Writing and Arithmetic**.

They realized that many of their kids were being indoctrinated with **Progressive** ideas disguised as a tenant of **Social Justice,** along with the need to recognize their inherent **bias** and the role it plays in keeping minorities from succeeding.

When you begin by telling a ten year old that they are **racist** by nature and that their parents and ancestors were **racist** before them, you are disrupting a young developing mind with concepts and issues that they should never have to deal with, and certainly not at such a formative stage in their development.

I've learned over the years, having worked as a teacher for a short time in my youth, that children, for the most part, do not see color. The younger the child, the less difference they see in other children.

Placing thoughts of **racism** into their minds can only create problems.

Forgetting the fact that children are not mature enough to deal with these issues, letting them begin to see differences that reflect **bias** can only result in confusion and ultimately, a sense of division that will lead to a less inclusive society.

Thanks to the pandemic, parents began noticing teachers trying to influence their children to accept either there oppressive heritage (white) or their state of constant oppression (minority).

Lenin would be proud.

Of course the **Progressives** deny all of it. They have **NO** classes that teach **Critical Race Theory**. The parents are being irrational and finding ghosts where none exists.

Thanks to these zoom classes, the revolution that is taking place in our schools and in front of our school boards indicate that the **Progressives** have woken the sleeping giant.

If you are looking for push back from the silent majority, you can't pick a better cause than the possibility of interfering with the proper development of our children.

So let me say thanks to the pandemic. I suspect that **American** parents will be watching things a lot closer than before, making it difficult for the **Socialist** among us to divide us further and use our kids to stoke the flames of **racism**.

Unfortunately a lot of damage has already been done, especially in the halls of higher education. We have convinced a significant portion of our college aged youth that **Socialism** is the answer to all of our problems.

COMMON SENSE MOMENT - Critical Race Theory

There's a famous quote that some have attributed to Winston Churchill. Whether he said it or not is less important.

What is important is that the true meaning of the quote has a lot to do with the value of experience in ones life. The more you experience the less you accept rhetorical nonsense as a substitute for known fact.

Here's the quote: "If you are not a Liberal when you're 25, you have no heart. If you are not a Conservative by the time you're 35, you have no brain."

Now the term Liberal in the early 20th century encompassed a lot more than it does today. The influence of Communism and the belief that the State was the answer to all things, reflected Liberal thought processes as Communism attempted to make their mark across the entire European landscape.

Churchill saw most bleeding heart Liberals as possible Communists and Socialists, thus influencing his opinions. Our present society has distinct differences between the extremes.

If the term Progressive was prevalent in his day, I would have no doubt that his quote, if he actually is responsible for it, would have been worded differently.

Sometimes it takes experiencing life for yourself in order to better understand that everything you hear and everything you are led to believe might not match up favorably with your experiences.

So it is with this dangerous, in my opinion, attempt at convincing us that Critical Race Theory is based on fact and reflects a truth about who we are that seems illogical to many of us.

What really matters is what your GUT tells you about this issue.

Does your Common Sense gene really believe that ALL whites are inherently racist because of sins that may have been committed centuries ago by some of their ancestors?

Does your Common Sense gene believe its possible for such a socially divisive concept as Racism to be passed on to future generations through their DNA?

There are still a significant number of people who believe this to be true and have called for black minorities to receive reparations

from our government because of past sins that they deem are responsible for keeping blacks from achieving their full potential.

In other words, they believe that our present generation, that has never held slaves, should pay retributions to the present minority generation, who never were slaves. Does Common Sense tell you this makes any sense whatsoever?

One look at our history should tell you that we have evolved considerably over the past two centuries.

There are no segments of our society that is not represented by a number of different minority groups, many of which have legitimate positions of power and influence.

How could that be possible if the majority of our population held biased and racist views? How would that work exactly?

No one can make the case today that minorities only hold positions of little importance, reflecting tokenism rather than acceptance.

If Critical Race Theory were true, the racist majority would never permit those they deem to be inferior, to achieve even modest levels of success, especially if it led to positions of power over the majority, such as elected office.

We all know that cannot be true. Our society and its political and business leaders, by their actions and the makeup of their institutions, tell us otherwise.

Cancel Culture

When the facts do not favor your positions, it requires extreme measures to shut down opposing views and alternative positions from seeing the light of day.

The **Progressives,** as stated on numerous occasions, use emotion to foster their agenda rather than fact, and that requires the rest of us to ignore our **Common Sense** gene by allowing our intellect to create a scenario that replaces reason with empathy.

- **All of those poor immigrants that are making their way to our southern border are fleeing for their lives from countries that are persecuting them and threatening them and their families. We are too kind a nation to refuse them asylum.**

- **Minorities in America are constantly being undermined by society and our law enforcement agencies. By using Racist tactics that prevent their advancement, including incarceration for minor offensives that would never be tolerated by non-minorities, they are being held back from achieving modest success in our society.**

- **The Electoral System in America is suppressing the minority vote by failing to provide sufficient opportunities for them to cast their vote. They do this by restricting the number of days and places for them to participate.**

- **The electoral system also limits the number of minorities who can participate by requiring highly restrictive measures to do so, such as photo ID's and a proof of Citizenship.**

- **Requiring such stringent methods favor the non-minority elements of society by asking for information that is not readily available to many in the minority community.**

None of these claims would survive a non-partisan **Media** that favored the facts over their political **bias**, however, that seems like a lost cause for the immediate future.

There remains a few **Media** outlets that are willing to buck the trend and present an alternative point of view but they are still in the minority.

While these alternative **Media** sources take a different path, they do draw a large audience and provide a buffer that has many **Americans** questioning the slanted versions that dominate main stream **Media** and **Big Tech** social and communication outlets.

Thus the need for a way to punish anyone that tries to support another point of view or dares to question the **Progressive's** position on anything of substance.

When anyone attempts to present an alternative position, they are accused of spewing **Misinformation or Disinformation**.

You hear these terms thrown around every day, especially from the **Media,** concerning any opinion that is not totally in line with the **Progressive** stance.

This is a blatant attempt at convincing average **Americans** that any opinion not in line with the government's must be flawed and without merit.

To believe this, you must accept that all of the government's positions are truthful and accurate. They are not.

Misinformation means that the position taken is inaccurate and reflects an incorrect interpretation of a fact.

Disinformation is actually a form of **LYING,** told to influence others to a false conclusion rather than the truth.

In both cases, they are assuming that the **Progressive** stance on anything is true and unquestionable. Do not question them or be chastised by everyone in power, including their mouthpieces in **Big Tech** and the **Media.**

Not having the facts on their side in most cases requires them to dish out some form of punishment or retribution to the masses who dare attempt to make use of their rights to **Free Speech**. Their weapon of choice is **Cancel Culture**.

The age of **Social Media** has transformed our society significantly and not always in a good way. We have instant information on just about anything occurring around the globe with the click of a button.

Unfortunately, many of the **Social Media** sites offer opinion rather than fact and identifying the difference is not as easy as one might think.

Our obsession with **Social Media** has led to a culture, especially among our youth, that spends most of their day looking at the tiny screen on their smart phones and searching a number of sites that provide for social contact among friends and social commentary from just about everyone, no matter the accuracy of those opinions and the validity of the source.

Cancel Culture has taken advantage of this new system of communication by harnessing the power of the medium. The **Progressives** understand this better than anyone.

We have all heard stories of how one highly tech savvy individual can pretend to be a mob by distributing a message as if the message was coming from hundreds, if not thousands of people, not just the one doing the transmitting.

This story is true.

The **Progressives** use **Cancel Culture** as a means of canceling anyone or any company that dares to disagree with their point of view.

We have seen hundreds of examples of this heinous use of **social media** to bring top celebrities, corporate entities and individuals that might still have a voice in our society to their knees.

An easy target for this mis-direction was our elite celebrities. Anyone that failed to tow the **Progressive** line was attacked in **social media** by hundreds of dissatisfied fans (probably just one or two) resulting in the loss of elite status in Hollywood.

Such a branding of displeasure led to a loss of job opportunities, failure to secure invitations to social events and the loss of that very important commodity known as **STREET CRED** by the elites in power.

The irony of this attack on the few that tried to take a more rational approach to social issues lies in how the entertainment industry remains among the most inclusive industries in the country.

It would be hard to find **biased** and **racist** practices anywhere in **Hollywood**.

They were among the first to integrate, the first to place minorities in keys roles and the first to offer minorities the opportunity to work both behind and in front of the camera.

All of their efforts on behalf of minorities were of little consequence when **Cancel Culture** came knocking. No one is permitted to have a different opinion if they were planning on maintaining their career.

You can only imagine how successful the **Progressives** were in **Hollywood**. A town full of superficial elite performers that are obsessed with their image and standing being ostracized for their less than enthusiastic opinions of the **Progressive** playbook.

They fell in line quickly and quietly.

I'm sure there are numerous members of the entertainment industry that are less enthusiastic about **Socialism** and more conservative by nature but the only path they have for continuing their careers lies in silence, so silent they will be.

Corporate America has seen their share of attacks due to **Cancel Culture**.

When companies start believing that thousands of their customers find them to be less **WOKE**, they show their dissatisfaction by speaking out against them and disrupting their business from multiple fronts.

It doesn't matter if their policies are rational, reasonable and non-threatening. If they do not follow the **Progressive** line, they are dangerous and need to be brought in line or **Canceled**.

Many companies began falling in line and that was one of the more disheartening aspects of the modern **Progressive Movement**.

I can only believe that these companies were hoping that their cooperation would protect them from future action that might affect their businesses.

However, I have no doubt that the ideology that is the **Progressive Movement** is too radical and I suspect that every one of these companies are just one misstep away from cancelation no matter their present efforts to cooperate.

They are choosing to ignore the basic principles of free enterprise in order to quiet the more radical left from selecting them to pay for the sins of non compliance.

In my opinion, alienating half the country in order to have a few minutes of peace will only come back to haunt you going forward. Just ask Disney.

Common Sense Moment - Where Angels Fear to Tread

I remember a time, not so long ago, when no company or industry discussed politics at all. It was the third rail of insanity to do anything that might limit their marketplace.

After all, if a company sold soap they hoped to sell it to everyone, not just those that favored a political point of view. Both Republicans and Democrats got dirty and they were both potential customers for your product.

Somewhere along the line, either due to their own stupidity or under pressure from Progressive politicians, many companies, athletes, entertainers and Media Outlets began changing the game and decided that many of us would, not only be interested in their political positions, but would be thrilled to hear them.

They ignored all of their instinctual warning signs, in other words their Common Sense gene, that told them that isolating one half of America was not a good thing for business.

Today, we have a level of insanity present in every industry that has led to nothing but lost business and outrage from a large segment of society that was totally avoidable.

Entertainers have lost fans, movies have suffered at the box office, companies have seen their profits begin to dry up and all of it was self inflicted, all because they were so convinced that all of America would see things the way they do and would praise their decision to let us hear what they had to say.

What I would give to go back in time and, once again, be in the dark as to the political leanings of any company or industry, and, if they are being honest, most of them would like the chance to do so as well.

COMMON SENSE MOMENT - Cancel Culture

What ever happened to our Freedom of Speech?

The history of our country was based on the foundation of the principle that every American had the right to their own opinions and the freedom to express those opinions, as long as they were not expressed in a dangerous or threatening manner.

While you could not cry FIRE in a crowded theater or threaten to kill another human being for expressing their views, you were

free to disagree with your fellow citizens, including the actions and opinions of your Government.

When was it dangerous to express any opposing views?

I have always believed that we have the right to both ignore the words and actions of others and choose another path, if we so desire. Preventing those opinions or actions from seeing the light of day was never an option. Why now?

The answer should be obvious when you choose COMMON SENSE over emotion by approaching this from a different angle.

According to the Progressives, an opposing point of view could lead to the possibility of having that view adopted by others, resulting in a number of opposing views being shared.

When you know that the only chance you have to succeed is to fool enough Americans into believing that emotion is a good substitute for fact, you cannot allow those opposing opinions to gain steam and infect other rational Americans with the message.

That requires Canceling that opinion before it can gain momentum.

The real test of the validity of a movement lies in the ability for that movement to survive all challenges and to come out on top in the end.

When you have no viable facts to support your movement, which is the case for the Progressive agenda, you need to stack the deck in your favor.

I truly believe that America would NEVER accept true Socialism as a way of life if they understood the history of its failures throughout the world and they understood the dangers in replacing individual rights and freedoms with a collective form of government that requires acceptance of outcomes over independent challenges.

Since we do not have a level playing field to choose our path,

we must fight back now and prevent the Progressives from altering our system of government by using a series of smoke and mirror techniques that would make Houdini proud.

The first step in taking the **Progressives d**own is to prevent them from indoctrinating our children. We must speak out whenever we see anything that suggests that our children are falling prey to their **WOKE** ideology.

When you turn these undeveloped minds decades before they reach the age of influence, you might not see the impact until years later.

Remember what **Lenin** said:

"***Give me just one generation of youth and I will transform the whole world.***"

CHAPTER NINE

Understanding the Progressive Influence

I'm old enough to remember a time, some decades ago, when both political parties were on the same page regarding many of the issues of importance to our citizens, including concerns about illegal immigration. Letting anyone into the country who did not go through the proper channels was considered to be problematic.

I can still hear **Democratic** politicians like Bill Clinton, Chuck Schumer, Joe Biden and many others looking for ways to stop the flow of illegal immigration, including the possibility of building a wall to protect our border.

All of that began to change when the **Progressive** element of the **Democratic Party** began to take hold and started influencing the direction that the **Democrats** would take on the political landscape.

The **Progressives** understood that you cannot convince free thinking people, who have enjoyed a lifetime of individual freedom, to consider giving it up in favor of government control without creating the proper motivation for changing the direction of the country.

In order to reimagine who we are as a country, they need to tarnish our present way of life and our system of government so as to open our minds to the possibility of change. Only then can they offer an alternative that might find support among a disillusioned citizen base.

Having the facts on your side would make the job a lot easier but that is not the case with the **Progressive's** push toward **Socialism**.

When your weapons of choice include emotional platitudes and misdirection, you cannot allow the facts to get in the way or your plans will be exposed for all to see, resulting in having your aspirations die on the vine.

The most surprising aspect of their takeover of the **Democratic Party** is how they managed to replace most of the moderate **Democrats** with far left acolytes that not only tow the party line but believe much of the nonsense that forms the base of the **Progressive** agenda.

The primary reason for this ideological change happening so quickly lies in their decades long indoctrination of our educational institutions that is beginning to take hold and pay big dividends.

Those early college students that first began to hear the value of **Socialism** from their professors are now in their **30's and 40's** and are in positions of power and influence throughout the **American** landscape. Most **Americans** never saw this coming.

How anyone could think that **Socialism** and government control was a path to a better life is beyond me. Don't they understand that government overreach means less personal freedom?

Are they aware that the more the government is responsible for, the less the private sector matters, and that places everyone in a very precarious position?

While many of our young and inexperienced citizens can be fooled into believing all of this nonsense, the more powerful among the existing **Democratic Party** cannot be fooled so easily, in my opinion.

All the older **Democrats** that have been in power for decades must be able to see through the **Progressive** ruse for what it is, a reimagining of a great and successful nation away from its **Capitalistic** roots.

This represents, in my opinion, one of the most disheartening aspects of the **Progressive Movement.** It proves the point that many politicians care less about their constituents than they do their own power and position.

After all, **Socialism** is not that bad when you are one of the **HAVES** rather than the **HAVE-NOTS**.

That alone should tell you just how little respect they have for our country, our citizens and our form of government, which has made **America** the most powerful and influential nation on the planet.

Everyone looks up to us for a reason and it begins with the sense of individual freedom that is not in abundance throughout most of the planet. We truly are a beacon of hope that lights the way for the rest of the world.

The **Progressives** want to change us from an independent and prosperous nation, in which they have limited control, to a nation of dependency with limited expectations, in which they have total control.

In spite of having no historical examples of previous success, they press on with claims of a better world and a fairer society under **Socialist** rule.

They are not blindly leading us toward a false **Utopia.** They know all too well that they are leading us toward less prosperity but that is the price one must pay in order to gain unlimited political power.

COMMON SENSE MOMENT - Why Socialism?

Do not be fooled by the Progressive message of providing for all Americans equally and fairly through Government intervention in all aspects of our lives.

I know of no historical example of Socialism, Marxism or Communism having succeeded in making anyone's life better or

fostering long term growth and prosperity for the nation under its rule, especially their citizens.

When the overall success rate is so abysmal, proponents must approach it from a different perspective.

The path they chose is to highlight a number of policy decisions that could appear attractive to the average person as long as the details remain hidden:

- *They talk about how wonderful FREE healthcare will be for all Americans.*

- *They try to convince us how fantastic it will be to provide FREE college to all young Americans looking to advance themselves and better provide for their future families.*

- *They promote the outstanding benefits that can come from allowing the government to support the less fortunate among us with stipends and FREE assistance programs that allow them to get by without having to provide the necessary effort and drive to accomplish things on their own.*

To the untrained eye, these can appear to be good things. It's just our benevolent government providing for its citizen in a meaningful way. How can anyone be against this?

This is where you need to activate your COMMON SENSE gene once again.

Just on face value, none of the services mentioned could possibly be paid for without extreme hardship on the tax payers of our country. That means financial restraints on EVERYONE, not just the favorite target of the Progressives, the wealthy.

Let's use the Healthcare example to take a trip into the weeds and get a better view of the details:

Do the Progressives ever explain how centralizing our entire healthcare system under government control might eventually lead to a level of care that is less than acceptable to most Americans?

- ***Why is Medicaid, our present system for the less fortunate, so problematic?***

- ***Why is Medicare, our system to aid our older population, who have paid into this system their entire lives, experiencing increased costs that require constant infusion of funds just to keep its head above water?***

- ***Why are a large number of physicians and Healthcare facilities refusing to take in Medicaid patients?***

- ***Why have drug companies refused to lower the cost of prescriptions to the levels requested by the government?***

The Progressives would like you to believe it all has to do with greed. While there is little doubt that greed plays a part in some of this, it misses the mark as the reason behind most of it.

Ask any medical professional that works under the Medicaid and Medicare system requirements. They will tell you how little the government is willing to pay for their services.

That forces the doctors and hospitals to see more patients, charge more for the services being provided under non-government insurance programs and limit the tests and preventive care being provided, that is now being done at a loss, in order to meet the unrealistic subsidies paid out by the government.

This is far from the panacea that the Progressives would like you to believe. Take away ALL of our healthcare options except for the government and you would have a system that might not be much better than average, at best.

The most profound issue resulting from total government control of healthcare would be the loss of alternative care options, no matter the cost, from our entire healthcare landscape.

Under government control, doctors would see their incomes slashed considerably and it might no longer be the path of choice as a career worth pursuing. That could lead to exceptional talent choosing other, more lucrative paths, rather than medicine.

Margaret Thatcher once said: "**The Problem with Socialism is that you eventually run out of other people's money.**"

Larger government and more control over our everyday lives is counter to the intentions of our **Founding Fathers**. They intended the **Federal Government** to be in place for the big things, not to grow so large as to be responsible for everything.

To simplify matters, on a global scale, they wanted the **Federal Government** to be the final line of defense as a protection from foreign invaders.

On the home front, they expected the **Federal Government** to protect our citizens from having their individual freedoms compromised by rogue States or over zealous politicians that interpret their election to office as some type of official mandate to place individual freedoms on the back burner of policy.

Can you think of anything run by our **Federal Government** that generates the necessary income required to keep them afloat?

With the unprofitable exceptions of the **Postal System** and **Amtrak**, they are a regulatory body that provides oversight for the private sector, education for the masses and military readiness to prevent foreign incursions, none of which earns us any income to offset their existence.

The money needed to run this country comes primarily from the private sector. They produce the goods and services that average **Americans** need, and are willing to pay for, that generates the tax base to keep us moving forward.

Socialism inhibits the growth of the private sector by eroding the value of our Free Market Society.

When the government is controlling the products and services, the incentives to create new and exciting services and revolutionary products that benefit our citizens begins to evaporate.

Finally, what no **Socialist** wants to admit or discuss is how just about **ALL** of our tax dollars need the private sector to earn the profits, hire the workers, pay their salaries and still maintain a profit significant enough to motivate companies to continue their operations and maintain their workforces.

If less people are employed by the private sector and forced to work for the government, where will the future incomes be generated that can pay for things?

COMMON SENSE MOMENT

Having any entity of power and influence, such as the private sector, that maintains our individual freedoms by creating jobs, opportunities and revolutionary products and services beyond the control of the government, is a danger to the Socialist Agenda.

It's hard to demand compliance when you have options that offer freedom of choice. In short, Capitalism is the enemy of Socialism, not just an alternative philosophy.

Karl Marx explained the battle between **Marxism** and **Capitalism** the best when he said:

"The last Capitalist we hang shall be the one who sold us the rope."

Why the Push for Illegal Immigration?

Before we answer that question, we need to take a step back and understand where the **Progressive** power base is the strongest and most influential. When you are trying to convert freedom loving **Americans** to your cause, you start with those that have less to lose and more to gain from **Socialism**.

You look to the inner cities that house a majority of the population that can benefit from social programs that might rob the people of their independence but rewards them with free stuff to offset that loss.

The fact that a significant number of lower income citizens, including large numbers of our minority population, can be found in many of the inner city communities, makes their job a lot easier.

When you do not have much to begin with, getting free stuff without having to work for it sounds like a pretty good idea.

What those that find **Socialism** attractive fail to notice is how these handouts rob us of our ability to choose and to work our way out of our present economic situation into a better one for ourselves and our family.

Getting handouts might seem like a good thing but living one's life based on such handouts guarantees that the chance to extract oneself from their present place in society is now much harder to accomplish and that is a sad state of affairs for the entire country, not just for those locked in poverty.

On a positive note, for those of us that are less than enamored with the **Progressive Movement**, they have seen a gradual degradation in support among the minority communities over the past few years, even as they hide behind the banner of the **Democratic Party**.

The **Latino** community, for example, has been slipping away from them for a decade or more while the **Black** community remains supportive, for the most part, with some exceptions.

Although the **Black** community still supports the **Democrats** in high numbers, they are beginning to see holes in their support popping up just about everywhere.

The last election in **2020** had the **Republican** candidate, Donald Trump, receiving approximately 13% of the black vote. That's almost double the support received just eight years earlier by Mitt Romney.

According to most political experts, that amount of minority support should have secured Trump a victory in 2020. I guess even the experts miss the mark on occasion.

This is where the immigration issue begins to make sense.

The **Progressives** have counted on minority support in order to win elections for years.

When they first noticed that they could not count on unwavering support over the last few decades, they decided that they needed an insurance policy so that they could nurture a new market that would help secure them election success for years to come.

That untapped market happens to be the increasing number of illegal immigrants, that will eventually have the impact they will require, once the Progressives can convince the rest of the country that they deserve the right to vote.

The first step in their plan is to flood the country with future potential voters for their cause, no matter the severe economic and social impact on the country.

Once Americans begin to accept these illegals as being viable members of society, they can start the process of finding ways to turn them into citizens, including all of the rights thereof.

Recently, we have seen a number of **Progressive** led States starting to allow illegal immigrants the right to vote in local elections under the guise that they are participating in electing people that will directly impact their lives as residents.

What part of illegal do they not understand? This is just the first step to allowing them to participate on a national level, which is the ultimate goal.

The **Progressives** would like us to ignore the fact that **America** has been a bastion of freedom for decades and one of the few countries that accepts hundreds of thousands of new immigrants to our shores, through legal and proper policies that foster immigration, not hinder it.

Unfortunately, our legal immigration system falls short of the millions needed to replace their weakening voter base. While they require millions more than the legal system allows, they need the majority to be less educated and with less resources at their disposal. Those lack of resources make them perfect candidates for entitlements and handouts.

As the **Progressives** bully average **Americans** into believing how these people are worthy of being a part of **America**, the hope is that they will remember which party supported them and vote accordingly, when given the opportunity.

The next step requires the loosening of border security so as to provide the motivation for many to make the journey, knowing that they have a better chance of making it into the country safely.

Since Biden's election, his **Administration** has been shouting from the rafters about how all of these immigrants looking to make their way to our borders are worthy of being taken in for a new and better life.

Why is anyone surprised that they decided to take him up on the offer and we now have millions of new illegals entering the country and making their way across all 48 contiguous states?

This is an important point for you to understand. The illegal immigrants are being shuttled all across the country by design, not chance. They need them to settle everywhere, not just in the **Progressive** cities that presently offer a safe haven.

They are well aware that our **Electoral College** provides a level playing field for national elections. Having more of the illegals settle in California, a state they already control, will not do them any good for a **Presidential** election.

They need all of the **RED States** and the **PURPLE States** to be inundated with newly adopted citizens that could alter the balance of power, and change that states political landscape to **Blue,** insuring long term control over our political process.

Time for a FACT LESSON

America is the land of opportunity and freedom that is the envy of the rest of the world, that goes without saying.

If we offered everyone across the planet the opportunity to enter **America**, without restraint, we would be outnumbered by new immigrants in less than a year. There are hundreds of millions of people that would rather live here than where they presently reside.

That does not mean that all of these immigrants that would rather live here are being persecuted in their present country, which is the standard line being presented by the **Progressives**.

In fact, over the previous decade, less than **10 to 12%** of those claiming asylum qualified as such. They were not being persecuted or in danger of losing their lives. They just wanted a better life here than they had there.

Why wait and attempt legal immigration when the borders are down and they can just walk over it and into the country without having to go through the arduous process of applying properly?

I doubt that there is any country on the planet that treats their borders with less respect and enforcement than we do right now. If you find one with a border as porous as ours, please let me know.

We are being lied to by the **Progressives** who need to bolster their support base in the future and have decided that illegal immigration was a viable means of achieving that result.

Once again, they choose emotion over fact.

While we have always been a refuge for many in times of need, we cannot forget that we are nation of laws. Those laws have a purpose and we are ignoring them in order to advance a political agenda that will alter who we are for decades to come.

Its time to open our eyes to what is really going on at our borders.

We are not saving the world's population from persecution, we are changing the landscape of **America** and, in the process, telling every immigrant that has followed the right path to become an **American** that they were foolish and naive to think that **America** valued their sacrifice.

Our **Vice President** is trying to convince us that all of these **asylum seekers** are coming from either Mexico or Central America.

She has taken on the assignment of dealing with, what the **Administration** considers to be, the root causes of our border issues by interacting with these governments and offering aid in order to raise their standard of living sufficiently enough to keep their citizens in place rather than having them attempt the journey in the first place.

However, the **Administration** prefers you remain in the dark about just how extensive this assault on our southern border actually is when those attempting to enter represent immigrants from hundreds of countries, not just a few to our south.

COMMON SENSE MOMENT

The last report I saw indicated that over 150 countries have had people entering the United States from our porous southern border. Our entire planet only has about 190 nations in total.

Many of these people traveled thousands of miles, mostly by plane, in order to arrive close enough to our border to cross it illegally under the guise of being a refugee.

Our Common Sense gene tells us that many of the world's population would prefer to live here rather than where they presently reside. That does not qualify them for refugee status nor should it.

Just wanting to go where things are better is not a viable reason to allow someone into our country without going through the proper channels.

The reason no other country allows such a porous border policy as ours needs to be addressed. Most countries understand the tremendous toll uncontrolled immigration has on their way of life.

There are two main concerns that can result from an open border policy with no viable checks and balances in place:

- ***Cultural Shifts***
- ***Economic Disruption***

Most countries have a great deal of pride in their cultural history, as they should. They have traditions, language and customs that need to be maintained that protects their citizens and their way of life.

We have seen our culture take a left turn over the past few decades that has changed our way of life and influenced our culture in ways that have been quite noticeable.

For example, while English is our national language, it is no longer our only language.

Speaking other languages is a good thing but that does not mean that Americans should be obligated to adapt to any foreign language in order to communicate.

When someone from another country decides to relocate to America, they need to adapt to our culture, not the other way around.

For a country to be successful and to prosper, every citizen needs to possess that all important attribute of love of country. Patriotism and its traditions and history needs to be preserved for future generations and it needs to be in full view for our existing generation.

Many of our newly acquired immigrant population, who have chosen not to take the proper path toward citizenship, seem to lack this attribute. They prefer continuing their previous culture and language and choose separation rather than assimilation.

That leads to an atmosphere that fosters less Patriotism, not more.

When you decide NOT to be a real American in every way, you lessen the resolve of the country and foster an indifference toward our country that will be a problem for us going forward, especially in times of war and civil disobedience, where strength lies in our unity, not division.

As for the economic impact that comes from uncontrolled immigration, our Common Sense gene should require little effort in this regard.

We are spending billions of dollars in tax payer funds to provide safety nets to new immigrants in spite of their legal status. Every dollar spent is one less dollar we have to help Americans or one more dollar of debt that our tax payers will have to endure for years to come.

The Progressives like to tug at our heart strings with emotional stories of how these immigrants were avoiding persecution and possible death in their home country but we know that is not accurate for the majority of people crossing the border.

The Progressives also like to tell us that these are all hard working people who will do the jobs that Americans do not want to do and they will be paying taxes just like the rest of us to offset their entitlements.

This is a STRAW ARGUMENT without facts.

The majority of illegals tend to work OFF THE BOOKS with no taxes paid whatsoever. The portion of illegals that are able to work on the books or who have stolen Social Security numbers in order to appear to be legal, might have money taken from their paychecks for taxes but unless they are in high paying positions, the tax burden is minimal at best.

We know from the available data that anyone earring less than $47,000 a year will pay minimal to no federal tax. How many of these unskilled immigrants crossing the border would fall into those income brackets?

In other words, the safety nets and benefits afforded most of these new residents far outweighs any contribution they might have to pay in taxes.

Our Common Sense gene should remind us that uncontrolled immigration has a far greater negative impact on our society than any benefit it claims to provide.

That's not a good thing no matter how someone tries to spin it.

We cannot emphasize this point enough. We are being lied to about the benefits that these illegal immigrants are providing to our country and our economy.

We are being lied to about their asylum claims, by pretending that most of our new arrivals to the southern border are in fear for their lives and are escaping from harm, much like the Ukrainians who are running from a war torn nation to a peaceful one in eastern Europe.

The biggest lie of all is that our southern border is not really an open border.

The fact that millions of people are being released into the country annually without proper vetting procedures counters the lies being told by our present **Administration,** which suggests otherwise.

There is a term that best describes a portion of these recent immigrants crossing the border; the **Got-a-ways.**

While our policy of non-existent border security has changed things to the degree that most of those entering the country are giving themselves up to the authorities, those carrying drugs or concerned that their identities might have them being held, are still avoiding the law and sneaking into the country.

Our **Common Sense** gene would suggest these **Got-a-ways** are not among the best and respected members of their country of origin.

We have already caught a number of known terrorists over the past few months and seized thousands of pounds of dangerous **Fentanyl** from reaching our population, but the numbers tell us that we are barely making a dent.

This year we expect to have nearly **2 million** illegals enter the country by giving themselves up to the authorities. The estimate given for the number of **Got-a-ways** is somewhere between **10-20%** of that number.

If we have stopped thousands of pounds of **Fentanyl**, how much got in?

If we believe as many as **200,000 to 400,000 Got-a-ways** will make it in without being caught, how many of them are criminals looking to do us harm?

Common Sense Moment - Got-a-Ways

Since most of the illegals entering through the southern border are finding their way into the country because of our open border policy, why are we still seeing hundreds of thousands of illegals sneaking over the border in order to avoid interacting with the border patrol?

Common Sense tells me its because they either have checkered pasts that will prevent them from being allowed to stay or they plan on being involved in unethical or dangerous behavior while here, such as drug related crimes, human trafficking crimes or terror related activities.

Let's remember that it was just a handful of terrorists that were responsible for 9/11 two decades ago. How many of these 200-400,000 Got-a-Ways need to be terrorists in order to create havoc in America?

We are being invaded for long term political purposes and that is far more important to the **Progressives** than having a safe and prosperous nation.

Until **America** begins to identify with the **Progressive** agenda of government control over individual freedom, cradle to grave entitlements over individual initiative and **Equity** for all replacing **Equality** of opportunity, they will maintain their pressure and work hard to break our will by forcing us to be dependent on government for just about everything.

The more they can be exposed for what they are, the better our chance to stop them in their tracks **BEFORE** we lose the power to do so.

CHAPTER TEN

A Cautionary Tale

The new age in **America** is one of speed and immediate gratification. Virtually nothing can happen of significance around the globe that we cannot learn about in minutes, if not seconds.

This is both a curse and a blessing.

Our children and grandchildren are experiencing things we could not even conjure up in our imagination. Most of these things are fantastic and rewarding while some are problematic.

All of us that have young children or grandchildren can attest to the fact that they do not see or interact with the world the way we do. Try getting them to talk on the phone rather than texting.

Most of them have no interest in television in the traditional sense, something that was a lifeblood for our generation. They are now streaming.

Broadcast TV and much of **Cable TV** is of no interest to them.

If I ever asked my grandfather about streaming, he would have gone into a long dissertation about the joys of fishing or taking a canoe down the river.

Companies like **Netflix** and **Amazon Prime** understood the changing world around them and began to alter our entertainment viewing habits to match the immediate gratification atmosphere that is now **America**.

Remember how we used to enjoy our television entertainment shows? Those that had our full attention became **"Must Watch"** television and we worked our week around the fact that we needed to be in front of the television when the next episode made its appearance.

We enjoyed the shows, talked about them with our friends, family and neighbors and waited patiently for the next episode to make it to our TV screen, especially early on, when there was no such thing as a **DVR** or a **VideoTape** option. If you missed a show, you missed it.

Our new streaming options understood the immediate gratification that was present day **America** and reacted accordingly.

They decided to develop the entire season of a show and release it all at once. This allowed our **WANT IT NOW** generation to spend hours, if they chose to do so, binging on one episode after another until the entire season was completed. Waiting for anything is not in their vocabulary.

As for the age of technology, I cannot even begin to keep track of all of the new and ever changing **APPS** that provide us with quick bytes of data and a means to communicate with others that has nothing to do with picking up the phone and talking to another human being.

These **APPS** are changing at a record pace as well. I recently found out that **FACEBOOK** and **TWITTER**, which I'm just starting to get the hang of, are no longer in vogue. It appears I missed the boat.

The younger generation has evolved toward better and quicker ways to interact that does not even require using all of the letters of the alphabet to complete a sentence or get another to understand their meaning. They speak in code, most of which I do not understand, leaving me in the dark, once again.

I thought that **TIC TOK** was the sound a clock made that was not digitally constructed. I found out it happens to be an **APP** that every young person in **America** under the age of thirty uses to entertain themselves.

The reason I'm belaboring this point has a lot to do with the fact that long term goals are less desirable than they used to be. Because of that, we fail to notice anyone still playing the long game. They become background noise and attract little interest.

Waiting for the right opportunity to present itself was an art that has little meaning in today's world. If you can't get immediate results, you might lose interest entirely or just decide to go on without it.

To their surprise, the changes occurring in our society provided a natural smokescreen that allowed the **Progressives** to remain in the shadows while they plotted behind the curtain.

The **Progressives** have been playing the long game for decades. Everything that has led us to this point in time has been planned out and nurtured along the way with the ultimate goal in mind; creating a **Socialist America**.

It's important to understand that, until now, the long game was the only game the **Progressives** had to play. They were not in power and had little support among those in power to push matters too quickly because of the fear of exposing themselves before all the pieces were in place for them to act.

The warp speed at which our world operates today provides them with the most protection possible. When you are looking for answers in minutes rather than over time, you are going to miss a lot.

I call that a version of the **"Forest for the Trees"** syndrome. We are so focused on our immediate needs that we miss the bigger picture that is forming right in front of our eyes.

Now that the **Progressives** have managed to reach the pinnacle of power, they have less reason to hide in the shadows. They can begin to put their agenda on a faster track and try to institute change while they have control over the outcome.

Make no mistake, they understand how radical their ideas are and that requires them to maintain a false front while attempting to change **America**.

Using the tools of misdirection and deception works just as well when you are dealing with a society that looks for quick answers and short term results.

If we do not actively oppose their plans with our actions and our voices, they will succeed in ruining the one nation on the planet that is benevolent and powerful enough to protect the freedoms of all nations who might need our assistance.

We have often heard about reaching a crossroad. Well, in my opinion, we are facing a critical crossroad right now.

If we allow the **Progressives** to make headway and begin changing the core beliefs that have propelled **America** to the country we are today, we may not be able to turn it around so easily.

We cannot be fooled by the **Progressive** claims that they are only looking to tweak things a bit, not change who we are as a nation.

When **Bernie Sanders** talked about Universal Healthcare being a **HUMAN RIGHT**, what he was saying is that choosing another path was less than **HUMAN** and that suggested a level of immorality on our part that needed to change.

When the **Progressives** talk about the need to provide advanced education to everyone, not just the rich, we are being lied to once again. Higher education has stopped being the domain of the wealthy decades ago.

In my opinion, they would have a better chance of convincing me that providing vocational training to everyone who chooses not to attend college was a goal worth pursuing. We need trained service personnel a lot more than we need college graduates who study the Arts.

When the **Progressives** try to convince us that **Social Justice** in not a form of **Socialism**, just the right thing to do for our less fortunate **Americans** who are not afforded the opportunities they deserve, we are being led down a path that only goes in one direction.

All of these issues lead to the destruction of **America** as we know it. Instead of being slaughtered outright, we experience death by a thousand tiny cuts.

- **When you overpay those out of work with excessive unemployment insurance, you devalue the person's need to work. In other words, you diminish one's drive and determination, key requirements to accepting Socialism over Capitalism.**
- **When you provide excessive welfare benefits with no stipulations, you take away the need to lift oneself from poverty, which leads to complacency, another requirement for a successful transition to Socialism.**
- **When you demand that entry level and part-time positions offer higher levels of pay than the positions warrant, you increase the cost of goods and services in the process. Sometimes a job at McDonalds is not meant to be a permanent position.**

Overpaying has consequences beyond the obvious, one of which is a sense of entitlement. The more the **Progressives** can foster the concept of entitlement in our citizens, the easier it will be for them to accept government assistance over their own sense of worth and the desire to succeed on one's own merits.

Socialism, at its core, leads to less opportunities for advancement and less chance for the individual to reach beyond their present role in society.

When the government is providing for you, there is less need for you to provide for yourself, even if by doing so you rise above your present status in order to achieve it.

Will **Americans** ever be happy with accepting who they are rather than striving for something better? I doubt it. Limiting our opportunities is not in our **DNA**. But first we must recognize the changes that are happening in front of us.

Diversity - Equity - Inclusion

The **Progressives** are very good at controlling the language. They claim to value **Diversity, Equity and Inclusion** above all else. Not surprisingly, you will have a difficult time finding any **American** that does not agree with the values attached to those words.

By controlling the language, they are in a better position to control the topic and put the rest of us who understand their deceptive tactics on defense rather than offense.

These three words are the central core of their message to the masses. They have been chosen carefully and with purpose. If they were being used in their proper context, everything would be fine.

We need to shine a light on their deception by separating the words and their true meaning from the distorted falsehoods that is the **Progressive** Agenda.

Diversity

Diversity is the acceptance and acknowledgement of a number of different things that can work in concert with one another. There is

diversity of thought, **diversity** of opinion and in the more tangible application, the **diversity** of culture and heritage.

Lately, we tend to tie the word **diversity** to **racial** issues, especially that of minority interaction with the white majority.

We are no longer in the age of Jim Crow or a time where slavery exposed the awful truth about man's inhumanity to man. Today, one just has to look around to know that **racial diversity** is being practiced everywhere.

The **Progressives** would like you to believe otherwise. They want us to dwell more on the past and to project past sins on to our present society as if nothing has changed over the past half century.

Progressives use the word **Diversity** as follows:

- **It always takes the form of a negative. They assume that the concept is lacking rather than flourishing.**
- **According to the Progressives, we need more diversity. They want us to believe that diversity is lacking in our daily lives, thus hurting those that are different from us in their skin color, cultural heritage or economic status.**
- **They want us to believe that American society is far less diverse than it really is. In fact, they want us to believe that we are dominated by a form of Supremacy of thought and action, most of which are targeted at minorities.**

Anything they can link to **Racism** is a good thing, according to the **Progressives**. The more they divide us, the better chance they have of changing who we are and who we perceive ourselves to be.

Diversity of thought is not only ignored but represents a threat to the **Progressives**.

Any opinion that differs from theirs must be silenced and demonized before it can gain traction. That's why their acolytes in the **Media** never promote stories that demonstrate how **America** successfully incorporates **Diversity** into our daily lives.

There are many such stories that never see the light of day. If a story might contradict their message, it must get as little publicity as possible. In other words, you will rarely find them celebrating anything we do that projects **Diversity** in a positive light.

Anyone that has read **The Art of War** understands how a successful battle requires that you divide in order to conquer. Without the strength that is found in unity, many will break ranks and the battle will be won by those who stand together.

Instead of using **Diversity** as an example of **American** tolerance, they use it as a weapon to divide us in order to force us to break ranks along **racial** lines, hoping to lead us down a path that will eventually destroy our **Republic**.

Equity

If the **Progressives** had nothing to hide, they would use the proper term that best exemplifies **America** and the **American Constitution** - **Equality**.

Their efforts, reinforced by **Big Tech** and the **Media**, to try and get us to believe that **Equity** and **Equality** are interchangeable, has been going on for years. We cannot allow ourselves to be fooled by their little language games or else we will be fooled into believing that their entire message must have merit.

For one last time, we need to correctly define these terms and pull the curtain back on the **Progressive's** need to distort the proper meanings.

Equality, in the sense that it is being used politically, is Equal Opportunity for everyone, no matter their race, creed, gender or economic status. No one can be denied the opportunity to succeed or to be included in society, no matter the source.

Equity is **NOT Equality**.

The **Progressive** definition of **Equity** stipulates that everyone, no matter their race, creed, gender or economic status has the right to equal outcomes, not opportunities. This is not how a meritocracy operates and that is the main point of creating the distortion.

Our C**onstitution** requires that every **American** has the freedom to choose the path they wish to take. They have the freedom to express themselves without fear of reprisal, as long as they do no harm in the process.

These freedoms allow all races, creeds and genders to choose a path of their choice and work toward achieving their goal of success. It does not guarantee outcomes or permit shortcuts that lessen the value of the goal.

You can choose to be a doctor or lawyer and a path is open for you to succeed, if you do the work and achieve the necessary prerequisites that are required of everyone who chooses those paths.

Can you imagine what problems would arise by permitting anyone the right to an equitable outcome who decides they want to be doctor or lawyer but has not taken the proper path?

That is what the **Progressives** are trying to do by proclaiming **Equity** instead of **Equality** as their direction of choice.

According to the **Progressives**, minority members of society have been overlooked and undermined for decades. They believe that its time they received equitable treatment, no matter the path they may have chosen, because the paths were being blocked and the opportunities were being denied to them all along.

The term **Reparations** is tied directly to the belief that **Equity**, as defined by the **Progressives**, needs to be the order of the day.

If not for our **Racial** bias and terrible historical history, all minorities would have been able to advance economically and socially in today's **America,** therefore they must be compensated for these inadequacies and the people who must pay for their failed **racial** policies are the present white majority.

Controlling the language can be a dangerous path to take and one that will guarantee that many **Americans** will be divided over issues that should never be on the table at all.

We are not the same country that permitted **slavery** to infiltrate our colonies and continue beyond our constitutional proclamation during the birth of our nation.

We are not the same country that decided to fight a civil war in order to enforce the principles of our **Constitution** for the entire nation, not just those that resided in the North.

We are not the same country that quietly and with purpose, permitted **bias** and **racial** discrimination to permeate our culture, while we pretended that it wasn't happening during the turbulent decades that was our nation post World War II.

The **Progressives** are well aware that we are not a **racist** nation. They know too well that a few isolated examples of **racial** prejudice do not reflect who we are as a nation. This is not a philosophical war around a difference of opinion.

This is an all out war on **America** that requires as many citizens as they can muster to fall for their fake interpretation of the word **EQUITY**.

If they can make a large number of **Americans** believe something that isn't there and pit them against the rest of the country that chooses to follow their own **COMMON SENSE** rather than falsehoods that spew hatred and division, they can sow the seeds of doubt that will help them to justify the need to change us into something that will be unrecognizable.

Inclusion

Here's a concept that should draw universal support. Just the thought of isolating any particular person or group from participating in the **American** dream seems like a nonstarter to most of us.

Unfortunately, this is another example of the **Progressives** controlling the language.

While they use the word **Inclusion** to explain their philosophy, they do so in an accusatory manner that suggests that **America**, in our existing **Capitalistic** society, is more exclusionary than our citizens realize or should accept.

Once again, they express themselves in a negative manner, intentionally avoiding all of the positive interactions and laws on the books that foster inclusion by highlighting actions that they can exploit for their purposes.

By claiming that they are in favor of including everyone fairly and equally in our society, they make sure that they imply the opposite is occurring, thus the need to point it out.

By claiming how one act of **exclusion** or **bias** represents our entire society, they unfairly paint all of **America** with a tainted brush.

It's under the guise of demanding inclusion that they wield their most dangerous weapon of all, **Identity Politics**.

Identity Politics

Have you noticed how just about everything coming from the **Progressive Left** is tied directly to identity?

- We need to have a **black** woman as Vice-President.
- Its time to have a **black** female Supreme Court Justice on the bench.
- There's not enough **women** in power positions in **Corporate America**.
- Its about time we had someone from the **LGBTQ** community in the Cabinet.
- The use of old and outdated pronouns to describe who we are such as **SHE, HER, HIM** and **HIS** are outdated in a **Progressive** society and must be replaced by gender neutral terms, no matter how confusing it will be to most **Americans.**
- **Transgender** individuals are more than their social identity, they are no longer the sex they were born with and we need to accept that as fact.

According to the **Progressives**, **EVERYTHING** is linked in some way to one's identity, which at its core, suggests the opposite of how we perceive the idea of inclusion. When you link everyone to an identity, you exclude them based on that identity.

Common Sense Moment - Gender Identity

Once you understand how the more divided we can be, no matter the issue or topic, you will begin to see the role gender can play in advancing the Progressive Movement toward their long intended goal line.

For my entire life, as I suspect yours as well, we were led to believe that all humans fell into one of two gender categories; male or female.

In fact, I doubt that any of us ever questioned the validity of that statement.

After all, biology is not open to interpretation and there are significant chromosomal differences that lead us to being a part of one or the other, never both nor some other gender yet to be discovered.

The Progressives use the term "Follow the Science" whenever it suits their needs. Whether true or not, it was their GO TO response when questioned about anything they chose to do during the Pandemic.

Today, we find that the unquestioned issue of biological identity is being blurred along social and political lines in order to deceive rather than enlighten, with the goal of widening the divide that binds us as Americans.

It appears as if they want us to believe that the ever expanding LGBTQ umbrella of alternate lifestyles reflect not just social and psychological changes but biological ones as well.

Let's take a step back, for the moment, to a time in recent history where this push for division along gender lines was non-existent.

Most Americans are tolerant of choices that individuals can make regarding their psychological and sexual preferences.

Let's take a moment of Common Sense clarity with this whole sensitive subject.

We have a significant Gay and Lesbian population that struggled obtaining acceptance in the beginning but that fight ended, for the most part, years ago.

We have a smaller segment that believes that they were biologically dealt a damaging blow by being born into a sex that does not properly align with their emotional and psychological

makeup, requiring them to alter their physical appearance to match who they are rather than what they are.

While these individuals, that fall under the banner of Transgender, are having a more difficult time adapting to society, as I'm sure society is to them, they have the added burden of making physical adjustments to their anatomy and appearance that warrants drastic modifications that make their journey from male to female, or vice versa, a lot more complicated.

Here's where the train begins to go off the rails.

I have no doubt that Transgender individuals, just like our Gay and Lesbian citizens, are totally committed to living their lives as they see fit, with their sexual preferences and psychological makeup intact.

None of these lifestyle preferences have anything to do with biology. Gay men do not believe that they are another gender other than male. The same can be said for our Lesbian women.

While our Transgender citizens are making physical changes to their appearance and anatomy, those changes do not alter their biological makeup that they entered the world with at birth.

The Progressives see this as an opportunity to position another wedge between us by intentionally blurring the lines between the sexes with the intent of suggesting that anyone who engages in physical alterations to their bodies are actually changing their biological make-up as a result.

When we have Transgender males, who are choosing to use the false claim that they have actually changed their biological makeup, being permitted to compete as a woman on the athletic fields and venues of women's sports, they are denying their true biological identity and creating physical disadvantages for their

women competitors, who are now at a disadvantage in the sport they love and have dedicated their lives to excel in.

Has anyone noticed that there does not appear to be many, if any at all, transgender females who are making the conversion to male, who are attempting to compete with biological males on the playing field? Could that possibly be due to them having less physical advantages in their corner?

Let's remember that in the world of science and medicine, there is no confusion along gender lines. If you need a blood transfusion or organ transplant, the new parts are categorized as either male or female. There really are no other options.

In other words, you can alter your appearance but you cannot alter your biological makeup that determined your sex at birth. We still only have two sexes that are in play for the entire human race. I doubt that will ever change.

We cannot let the Progressive Movement, along with their WOKE acolytes and their Cancel Culture army of warriors, bludgeon us into submission by pretending that we are more than our biological birthright when it comes to gender physiology.

That does not diminish the fact that all of these alternative lifestyle choices have merit and deserves tolerance and inclusion in our society.

We are a tolerant nation, for the most part, but that does not mean we should allow radical groups a platform to force us into believing something that is not true, just so that they can change attitudes along false lines of delineation.

Letting biological men compete with women will lead to the end of women's sports as we know it. That does nothing but place one class above another and diminishes the role women play in our society, something we thought we have overcome decades ago.

Pretending that a man can give birth to a child, a physical impossibility, does not represent a rational approach to society just because someone says it does.

If a transgender male chooses to have a baby, thanks to their biological makeup, they might be able to do so. Does that mean that a man is able to give birth? What it actually suggests is this transgender male has accepted their biological nature for a specific purpose; nothing more, nothing less.

All of this gender identity push by the Progressives has just one goal in mind, pitting one American against another for the purpose of weakening our will to resist their end goal of changing America from who we are to who they want us to be.

Identity Politics along Racial Lines

Martin Luther King would turn over in his grave at the suggestion that **African American** citizens be treated differently because of their ethnic identity. He always preached absolute inclusion, not the type that highlights ones differences and attempts to treat them with special benefits under the guise of inclusion.

The last thing we need to do is to highlight **African Americans** based on the color of their skin rather than the fact that they are no different from the rest of our **American** citizens. Separating the black community because of their race would be the last thing **Martin Luther King** wanted to see happen.

The **Progressives** see this differently. They see **Racial Identity** as another tool for them to foster division.

They want us to think that we are back in the fifties once again and that the **Systemic Racism** that lives beneath the surface is working to sabotage one **Race** for the benefit of another.

Does your **Common Sense** gene tell you that this argument has any merit?

Example of Inclusion and Identity Politics - Our Electoral System

When the **Progressives** talk about the need to include everyone in our election process, no matter their race or creed, that suggests that our present system is falling short of accomplishing that objective.

When they try to pretend that our election laws are suppressing the vote of certain members of our society, they want us to believe that our election laws are **exclusionary,** thus the need to overhaul them for the good of the nation.

Instead of suggesting that our laws exclude the poor or less educated among us, they claim it has more to do with **Race** than economic status. In other words, the election system is **Racist.**

Why we would have laws or procedures on the books that hinder a certain identity from exercising their rights is beyond me but that is their claim. According to the **Progressives**, the racial overtones are subtle and hidden from view, but they are there nonetheless.

To me, that may be the most **racist** thing I have heard in a long time.

If it's only the **black** community being hurt by voter **ID** laws or limited voting hours and locations, the **Progressives** are intimating that the **Black Community** lacks the tools or the where with all to access the tools necessary to meet the election requirements.

If our laws do not stipulate ethnic differences, how can just one identity be impacted by these supposedly exclusionary laws?

Be that as it may, what is the **Progressives** suggestion to alleviate this?

They would like us to change our election laws to accommodate those incapable of meeting the requirements by eliminating the voter **ID** laws, along with the necessary step of verifying citizenship, for all **330** million **Americans** living in the **United States,** in order to rectify this perceived fault in our system.

To date, the **Progressives** have failed to identify **ONE** such citizen that is successfully functioning in society without a proper form of identification.

They have cited no examples of restrictive hours or deceptive practices that deny citizens the opportunity to vote. In other words, these are claims of emotion with no discernible facts to back them up.

Based on nothing of substance, they want to change our election process that has worked for centuries. Could it be that they have another, less obvious reason for turning our elections on its head?

The **Progressives** are fully aware that their plan to turn **America** into a **Socialist** country will not play well with most of our citizens once exposed for what it is, therefore, they need to have as much control over the election process as possible.

The present system of voter **ID** and proof of citizenship limits their control and that leaves them too vulnerable on election day.

They managed to convince our nation that the pandemic would keep everyone home so mail-in ballots were necessary on a large scale. Their success in the 2020 election suggests that the lack of control over the ballots being sent through the mail help lead then to an unexpected victory.

If they can maintain the need for mail-in ballots and eliminate the added restrictions of **ID** and Citizenship verification, who knows what benefits that may lead to in future elections?

There's no reason for you to attempt to look behind the curtain.

Just remember that our **Progressive** leaders are in favor of **Diversity, Equity** and **Inclusion** and leave it at that.

COMMON SENSE Moment - Diversity, Equity and Inclusion

Diversity

While there are always isolated examples of all types of behavior on display in a country as large as ours, we cannot be defined by isolated examples.

We are not a racist country that fails to promote Diversity.

You would be hard pressed to find any significant examples of outright racial policies that permeate any industry, educational entity, athletic outlet or religious affiliation with a tangible lack of diversity in both their requirements or their actions.

To pretend otherwise is not only deceptive but morally reprehensible.

Our Common Sense gene knows that we are a diverse society that incorporates all races and genders throughout society and that could never happen if we were closet bigots who preached diversity but did the opposite behind closed doors.

A lack of Diversity on a grand scale, as suggested by the Progressives, could not be hidden from view. It would infect society in such a way as to expose its prejudices for all to see.

We are not an extension of every isolated incident that lacks diversity as if that act exposed the real America rather than showing us that every nation remains a work in progress.

Don't let anyone suggest we are a nation that remains less diverse than our ancestors. When that claim is made, make them

prove it, not with an isolated example, but with proof of infestation on a grand scale.

I know they will be at a loss for words.

Equity

The best way to dispute this play on words is to ask those who profess the need for a more equitable solution to first define the meaning of Equity.

Does anyone who uses Common Sense believe that those who lack the necessary expertise or skill set to do a specific job ought to be given that job?

Does anyone really believe that white immigrants to this country from poor ancestral backgrounds should pay reparations to anyone for their historical past? If so, they should be in line as well.

My Irish relatives who came to America because they had no opportunities or means to feed their families back in Ireland at the turn of the last century never owned slaves or had more than a few nickels to rub together when they landed in this country. In fact, they were little more than slaves themselves back in Ireland as they struggled for survival.

There are millions of Americans whose relatives have similar stories who landed here with nothing of substance to their names except the desire and work ethic to give their families a better life.

Is there anything in their past that suggests that they were privileged individuals who benefited from the misery of others?

I'm sure our ancestors would have loved to be given opportunities beyond their limitations but that is not how things work. You overcome your deficiencies and learn the skills necessary to reach beyond your humble beginnings.

Our Common Sense gene tells us that equitable treatment, resulting in unearned outcomes are just another name for handouts. The more we get without having to earn it, the less motivated we are to earn anything.

Equity is a manufactured trap that can only lead to less inclusion and more division. By using our Common Sense, we can avoid falling into that trap and we can help others from falling into it as well.

We are blessed by our Founding Fathers with a doctrine that promotes Equality. Do not let anyone tell you that Equality and Equity are synonymous.

Inclusion

It is terrible how our nation continues to exclude certain members of our society from getting ahead.

Because of our exclusionary policies, women and members of ethnic minorities have been unable to gain a foothold and prosper under our biased and prejudicial societal norms.

That's what the Progressives who like you to believe.

However, exposing obvious examples of this lack of inclusion are difficult to find, except for the isolated example that every society encounters from time to time.

Common Sense tells us that a lack of inclusion is not systemically part of the American Culture.

For that to be the case we would have numerous roadblocks placed in front of the minorities that they claim are being excluded from succeeding and that requires tangible proof, not innuendo.

To sum up our **Common Sense** look at the **Progressives** and their moral belief in the need for Diversity, Equity and Inclusion:

- ***The only interest they have in Diversity is to point out the lack of it. Pretending we are less diverse is another way for them to paint us with the brush of Racism, a necessary tactic to divide us further apart.***

- ***Trying to convince Americans that Equity and Equality are synonymous is a plan that will lead to further division. Americans will resent having to give opportunities or reparations that are not earned and rightfully so. How can division not flourish under such a system?***

- ***By pretending a lack of inclusion, the Progressives are furthering the false innuendo that America prefers to be exclusionary, which can only serve to divide us further and more expansively, as we are not only excluding along racial lines but along gender, ethnic and educational lines as well.***

What a terrible country we have become if we are to believe any of this nonsense.

Under the guise of creating a new society for the better good, **Progressives** are destroying our way of life and hoping we will thank them in the end.

Daniel Webster said it best when he warned us how political power could lead to a loss in freedom for the masses:

"Good intentions will always be pleaded for every assumption of authority. It is hardly too strong to say that the Constitution was made to guard the people against the dangers of good intentions. There are men of all ages who mean to govern well, but they mean to govern. They promise to be good masters, but they mean to be masters."

Just remaining silent, while we stay in the background of cultural change, is no longer acceptable. We must find a way to make our voices heard.

We have the facts on our side and with the help of **Common Sense**, we have the opportunity to bring like minded citizens along for the ride.

The **Progressives** are counting on our desire to play fair and avoid conflict, while they attack and wage war on our way of life.

Its time to fight back.

CHAPTER ELEVEN

With the **Progressives** finally finding themselves in a position of power, they needed a plan to begin making policy changes that would lead us down the road to **Socialism**.

There are a number of policies that hide their true intent but will eventually get them where they need to be, on the cusp of altering **America** to better reflect their power based, government control social agenda.

We need to see what is behind the mask they place in front of our eyes and ears, and resist their efforts while we still can.

Here's a list of some of the policies that are designed to foster their long range movement toward Socialism:

Matching Policy Changes to Socialistic Outcomes

ISSUE

- The **Progressives** managed to separate us from energy independence, leaving us beholden to other nations for critical energy resources that, no matter the claims of the **Climate Change** advocates, is the key to global power and dominance, and will remain so for decades to come.

A Common Sense Look at this Issue

Energy is one of the keys to America's successful role on the world stage.

It represents our superior position among energy producing nations and stands out as one of the more successful results of a well run Capitalistic Society.

Energy independence represents freedom for America on the world stage. The more freedoms we have the less chance the Progressive have of getting us to accept government control over personal responsibility, making energy independence a serious threat to their plans.

In order to knock us down a peg and leave us less independent, it became necessary to remove us from the top position and allow our economic future to be one that is not totally American driven.

When we became, for the first time in half a century, totally independent for our energy needs from foreign sources and a main exporter of energy around the globe, it was such a triumph of Capitalism and American ingenuity that it threatened the Progressive Movement to the extent that they made it their main point of contention when given the power to do so after the 2020 election.

The path to accomplishing that objective lied with the false claim that Climate Change was an immediate threat to our well being and that America needed to lead the way, no matter the economic price we had to pay, in order for the world to follow our example and get on board.

All of the facts and evidence that were contrary to that belief, needed to be silenced and ridiculed so that the average American could not hear an opposing view, especially one that was rational and sane with an abundance of factual support behind it.

It was not an accident that the President threw the first punch within hours of being sworn into office, with the canceling of the Keystone pipeline that cost more than 70,000 good paying jobs and prevented a safe and secure method of transporting millions of gallons of oil a month from Canada to the United States.

The added regulation restrictions and canceling of drilling permits across the country almost immediately led to a dramatic reduction in available energy, virtually eroding our energy independence in months, something no one thought possible.

One of the most damaging attacks on American energy was the negative stigma the Administration placed on all Fossil Energy, including the push for the lending institutions to deny easy access to funds for anyone looking to finance a new well.

Today, the Administration pretends that there are still thousands of leases not being acted upon by the energy producers, as if the lack of production is by choice, not directive. A lease is not a permit to drill.

When it costs millions to even prime a well with no guarantee of success and you are being told that the banks, who usually fund these long term investments are no longer comfortable doing so, you are impeding the one industry that can help us maintain our superiority on the world stage by preventing them from maintaining their present levels, much less expanding.

No matter what our politicians say, or what our Media tells you about the energy industry, the threat the energy industry poses to the Progressive agenda is too dangerous to allow it to prosper and that is why we are less energy proficient today. Americans are left with a high price to pay for their ideological directive as their

actions have all of us paying a steep price at the pump and in our homes.

ISSUE

- The **Progressives** managed to reverse the best economy our nation has seen in more than forty years and position us in the middle of an inflationary curve that has all the signs of becoming an actual **recession**.

A Common Sense Look at this Issue

America had their best economy in over sixty years, with exceptional growth in all aspects of our society, from employment among all societal and racial groups to a level of corporate investment in growth that was lacking for decades.

While the Pandemic managed to halt our economy in its tracks for months, the core elements that made it so successful were still in place and ready for us to rebound and prosper once the threat was over.

The Progressives would like all of us to believe that the tax cuts that helped us to reach those welcome levels of prosperity were really only handouts to the rich and powerful.

While that is blatantly false, since every working person in this country had their family income increased significantly, they chose to ignore the number one reason why our economy needed to be resurrected in the first place; an overabundance of regulations.

Every industry had their hands tied for years because of restrictive regulations that either prevented them from expanding their businesses or punished them too harshly with environmental

claims that their actions interfered with the goal of achieving a carbon neutral nation.

Replacing the massive regulations that were cut by the previous administration was at the top of their list of things that needed to be done. Within months of taking office, Corporate America was no longer free to operate and expand their businesses.

It's hard for a company to think of expansion when the government places unrealistic roadblocks in front of them at every turn.

High on their list of changes is renewing the stifling tax burdens for having your corporate headquarters in the United States, another key factor that, once these taxes were lessened, led to our previous economic windfall.

The last thing we need is to have American companies headquarter in foreign lands in order to prevent necessary profits from being swallowed by government overreach.

In an effort to tie the hands of our Capitalistic economy, the Progressives failed to understand just how impactful these restraints would be on our entire country, not just a few isolated industries that were in their crosshairs. Their lack of business acumen led to terrible inflation quicker than they realized.

Did they understand that paying people to stay home rather than working would lead to more jobs going unfilled in our nation than any other time in our history?

Did they consider how this shortfall of employees would leave every restaurant, hotel, trucking company, manufacturing facility and shipping company with less personnel to function properly?

When you have less people to do the job, you get less productivity. Less truckers and shipping personnel means shortages in getting goods to market. That leaves store shelves empty and profitable companies in danger of a loss of business that might lead to failure.

Did they understand that just about everything we manufacture and many of the services we require depend on fossil fuels? It's not just the price of gasoline for our cars. It's more complicated than trying to get every American to buy an electric car.

It takes more than a directive to use less gas and oil to reconfigure every home in America away from fossil fuels in order to keep their families warm in the winter.

Do the Progressives really understand that America is decades, if not centuries away from eliminating fossil fuels in some form or another? With no plan in place to accomplish such a sea change, they are leaving us with no where to turn and no money to afford the journey.

Inflation is complicated and a result of a number of things, not just one. Their simplistic attempt at getting us to change without a viable direction that will work for us, is more than just delusional, its demonic.

Americans are suffering with the rise in prices and the loss of supply and unless we find a way to lower the cost of energy and stop paying people to stay home, we are going to fall into a recession of massive proportions while remaining on a dangerous road.

That road toward depression, something we have not had to endure in nearly a century, would not just knock us off the perch of global dominance but leave us open to numerous attacks from nations that want to seize the opportunity because of our weakened state.

I hope that Americans can see, with their own eyes, how the Progressives have overplayed their hand. We cannot allow them to

fool us into believing that all of this pain and sacrifice is required in order to protect the climate.

Climate issues are global, not national. One nation can never make a significant dent in such a monumental issue alone.

To believe that our sacrifice will motivate or embarrass other nations to change their ways is nothing short of delusional. To claim that we are all going to die if Americans fails to alter their way of life quickly and totally in the next few years is insane.

To admit that all of this nonsense is just a ploy in order to get us to abandon our Capitalistic system of governance in return for a Socialistic system that is more environmentally acceptable, is a form of madness.

ISSUE

The **Progressive** mishandling of **International Affairs** has so badly left us vulnerable to a number of bad actors that see us weak and without the necessary resolve to properly preserve freedom and democracy when it is threatened anywhere on the planet.

A Common Sense Look at this Issue

The first place to look for a lack of international competency is our withdrawal from Afghanistan. While most Americans preferred that we end this occupation and bring our soldiers back home, no one could possibly believe that we left properly and to the best of our ability.

Common Sense should tell us that we were in the driver's seat in Afghanistan and we could choose when and how we left and under what terms that withdrawal would take.

After all, we had the military might in country to back up our planned withdrawal and if you add in the fact that our enemy, the Taliban, would like nothing better than to see American troops leave the area, it would be a terrible move on their part to interfere at all.

Why fight battles you cannot win when your enemy has already announced that they were leaving?

Over the span of twenty years, we had thousands of Afghan support personnel in country that assisted us on many fronts in our battle to rid them of their mortal enemy.

Unless the Afghan Army could maintain control, once we left, which turned out to be a pipe dream, we had an obligation to these supporters to remove them and their families from country in order to save their lives. The Taliban were not known to be merciful and any supporter of America would be an enemy of the Taliban.

The Administration's decision to begin withdrawal by first removing the military was nothing short of insane. Who could rationalize that taking out our defensive forces first would make the process easier and less problematic?

While we may have spent twenty years trying to create an Afghan army that were up to the task of keeping the Taliban at bay, our military experts must have known how slim of a possibility that would end up being.

So we ignored their ineptitude, left them billions of dollars in high tech and advanced weaponry and equipment and then, as a final gesture of incompetence, pulled all of our soldiers out before we began evacuating our citizens and our Afghan partners, hoping against hope that the Afghan Army would be successful in having our backs instead of our own troops.

As a result, the Administration left thousands of Afghan

partners behind to fend for themselves, along with a number of Americans, while pretending that they were responsible for the largest evacuation mission in history. In the aftermath, our Administration and the Media failed to tell our citizens that they evacuated the wrong people.

Another example of international ineptitude has us negotiating with the number one terrorist state on the planet, Iran, to re-establish the former nuclear deal that would guarantee us that Iran would be a nuclear country in a few short years.

Since Iran has chosen to refuse to sit down with us, the Administration has arranged for Russia to be our intermediary and allow them to strike a deal on our behalf.

The same Russia that is presently invading their neighbor Ukraine, causing untold death and destruction, including numerous war crimes, by targeting innocent citizens as they try to bomb them into submission.

Could it be feasible that we are not doing everything possible to protect human life in Ukraine because we owe a debt to Russia for their ongoing negotiations with Iran?

Let's be clear, the world knows that America seems to lack the resolve necessary to take on any difficult task around the globe. Will that lead China, Iran, North Korea and other bad actors to flex their muscles during a time when America seems less inclined to flex theirs?

Only time will tell.

ISSUE

The **Progressive** policies have created a disaster at our southern border that has seen millions of new illegals making their way into our country unimpeded and with little oversight.

A Common Sense Look at this Issue

There is very little about the flood of illegals entering our country from our southern border that makes any sense. We already have a robust immigration program that takes in more new immigrants per year than just about any other country on earth.

Common Sense suggests that this is being done because of reasons that are not easily understood or the Progressives would have successfully made their case a long time ago.

We already know the majority of illegal immigrants are not in fear of their lives.

We already know that conducting a proper and comprehensive vetting process is impossible under the circumstances and that would require a desire to do the proper vetting in the first place.

We already know, based on the number of sanctuary cities throughout the country that promise to provide a safe haven from our laws and our law enforcement personnel, that they are well aware that these newly arrived immigrants are breaking the law.

Has anyone ever provided us with a viable reason for allowing this assault on our border to take place?

We already know, based on past history, that the majority of people entering illegally are not eligible for Asylum status.

Are we to believe that it is a good idea to open our borders to anyone that would rather live here than where they presently live?

If that is the reason, then you can kiss our country goodbye as we will be overrun within the next few years with more people than we can possibly accommodate.

At the present rate of influx at the border, by the end of Biden's 4 year term we will have more illegals entering our country than the entire population of Texas.

Does your Common Sense gene tell you that is okay?

The Progressives know all too well that this attempt at creating a new voter base for their long range plans to remain in power would not sit well with present voters, thus the need to lie that our border is really not being overrun.

ISSUE

The **Progressive** support network, that consists of the **Media** and **Big Tech**, has begun to erode a vital key to our success as a nation.

We are lauded around the world for our freedom of speech, freedom of choice and our unalienable right to life, liberty and the pursuit of happiness. These principles are being attacked on a daily basis and little, if anything is being done to combat it.

A Common Sense Look at this Issue

Our Founding Fathers and the Constitution made a pretty big deal about protecting our Freedom of Speech.

It was placed right at the top of their list because it was the one thing that was missing from British Rule that left most of our citizens without a voice in matters that were important to them.

The Progressives never claim that they are involved in any form

of suppression but that is exactly what is happening right under our noses.

How may you ask?

Under the guise of preventing dangerous comments from reaching the masses, the Media and Big Tech have decided that you are not permitted to see anything that might be classified as "Misinformation, Disinformation, Hate Speech or Dangerous Rhetoric".

Today, we see student bodies from many of our colleges and Universities preventing anyone with an opposing point of view from expressing their opinions on campus.

This is not just an isolated case. Even law students at one of the more prestigious law schools in the country prevented conservative speakers from talking on campus at a "Free Speech" seminar.

Does anyone else see the irony when students that choose to use their own Free Speech rights are using their rights to silence someone else's Free Speech rights?

According to the Progressives, what qualifies as Speech Crimes that warrants censorship?

Here's where everything goes off the rails.

Big Tech has come up with a system that is designed to spot problematic speech that, they claim, is being monitored by computers and are not subjective in any way. They call these monitoring programs Algorithms.

Whenever these algorithms identify content being posted by anyone that falls into their pre-selected category they deem problematic, the computer blocks the posts and issues either a warning to the person posting it or actually suspends the writer's account for unauthorized postings.

They claim that this is an arm's length process that takes the human element out of it so as not to allow bias to enter into the decisions.

Question: Doesn't these algorithms have to be programmed and created by fellow humans with their own potential bias having a say in the creation to begin with?

We can no longer allow Big Tech to hide behind these human generated algorithms. They are intentionally limited and they are blocking our Free Speech rights on a daily basis while we sit back and allow it to happen.

What these algorithms actually do is flag ANY speech that does not agree with the Progressive point of view and that constitutes suppression of our unalienable Freedoms.

Here's a perfect example of an average American having their opinion blocked because it does not agree with the Progressive point of view on this topic.

Example

Big Tech, in this case Linkedin, censored an Air Force veteran by the name of Gretchen Smith for posting about her journey from poverty to becoming a College graduate.

It appears she had the nerve to complain about the government's position on removing tuition debt for millions of students around the country.

Here's the exact post. Tell me what your Common Sense gene says about the dangers of having this post blocked from being seen by fellow Americans because of its content?

Did I tell you that it was flagged by one of those algorithms that identified it as HATE SPEECH and worthy of blockage?

"I am not responsible for your student debt. I grew up in poverty

in NC, ate from a garden, my name was on a community Angel tree for Christmas, I bought clothes from yard sales & if I was lucky, on a rare occasion Sky City. I joined the Air Force then went to college. I made it happen."

Because she had the nerve to disagree with the concept of paying for another's tuition expenses, she was accused of Hate Speech and blocked from the website.

We are allowing our Media and Big Tech communication networks to prevent us from exercising our rights under the Constitution and that represents one of the most dangerous and prohibited warning signs that we are no longer free to express any opinions.

Sounds a little like how King George treated America before the Revolution.

Here's a good place to remind everyone what one of our Founding Fathers thought about the importance of Free Speech:

Benjamin Franklin

"Printers are educated in the belief, that when men differ in opinion, both sides ought to have the advantage of being heard by the public. For when truth and error have fair play, the former is always an over match for the latter."

ISSUE

We have always been among a rare handful of nations that approached Law and Order without political interference of any kind.

That is changing rapidly as the **Progressives** have managed to strategically place a number of key **District Attorney's** and **Progressive Judges** in positions of power who believe that our laws are flawed, thus they choose to ignore them on a grand scale, in favor of what they call a more acceptable way of addressing **Social Justice** in **America**.

A Common Sense Look at this Issue

One of the worst things that can happen in America is to politicize our system of Law and Order and remove the barriers that protect us from those in society that have chosen a different and more dangerous path.

We have prisons for a reason and the law never asks anyone their personal and political leanings. Break the law and you pay the consequences or, at least, that is how it used to work.

The Progressives in power have interfered with our law enforcement system by placing political hacks into positions of power that see the law as an option rather than an absolute.

Since they view our laws as being little more than suggestions, they can decide, based on their own beliefs, what laws to enforce and what laws to ignore.

They would like you to believe that our Systemically Racist nation has already skewed the law to favor the white majority and they need to correct those racist policies by ignoring the law and changing the outcomes for thousands of criminals that are victims of our system, pretending they are not actual criminals but victims of circumstance.

With thousands of hardened criminals placed back on the streets by these WOKE officials, we are no longer safe in our own homes or on the streets of our hometown.

Common Sense tells us that multiple felonies by a single criminal

is not a result of racist laws. Placing dangerous felons back on the street can only lead to more crime, a higher number of deaths, increased injuries and more assaults.

Every person in jail is not there because they stole a loaf of bread to feed their family. Don't let anyone tell you otherwise.

There is some Good News coming out of the Progressive playbook that has resulted in a few hiccups.

Since the **Progressive's** rise to power, two major issues were massive enough so as to prevent the **Media** from either spinning them or ignoring them.

Thanks to the national exposure, our citizens were able to see behind the curtain, something the Progressive's preferred we never see:

- **Our withdrawal from Afghanistan**
- **Our recent bout with Inflation**

Afghanistan

The horror associated with our withdrawal from **Afghanistan** could not be kept from the masses. When you can observe disaster with your own eyes, its difficult to spin it as a good thing, no matter how hard the **Media** tried to do so.

The **Administration** tried to turn abject failure into triumph by evacuating more than **100,000 Afghans** that were part of the crowds that stormed the airport, pretending that all of these people were properly vetted and were among the targeted **Afghans** that assisted us over the years. Our eyes and ears told us a different story.

They needed numbers to show their resolve and they took anyone in the vicinity of the planes that were supposed to carry our **Afghan** partners and citizens to safety.

As we have said earlier, leaving thousands of **Afghan** partners behind, along with a number of **American** citizens, created one of the more horrendous human rights failures in our history.

Adding to the disaster, the inexplicable decision to abandon **Bagram Air Base** along with **billions** dollars in military weapons and equipment, made no sense to the average **American**, no matter what the **Media** spun in their direction.

A person does not need to have a military background or strategic war training to know that the military are always the last to leave if you want to protect your people in the process of evacuating.

When you botch something this big, our entire country observed the disaster that was **Afghanistan** and the **Progressive** partners in the **Media** and **Big Tech** were not able to hide the mistakes or spin it successfully.

That alone, in my opinion, led to a dramatic decline in favorability for the present **Administration.** As to whether the **Media** can find a way to turn those numbers around in time for the next election, time will only tell.

Inflation

That leads us to the second issue that has hung a heavy weight around the necks of the **Progressives**; the impact that **inflation** has on our economy.

Finding themselves in a position of supreme power for the first time, one can understand their desire to act quickly and concisely to turn the tide of **Capitalism** and pave the way for their **Marxist** agenda to take hold.

When they began by declaring war on our energy industry under the guise of **Climate Change,** they set in motion a series of economic disasters that took a downward spiral, leaving average **Americans** in a tight spot with serious financial problems that could not be ignored.

Because we may be on the verge of extinction, or so they claim, it was necessary to eliminate the primary threat to humanity as quickly as possible, which was our dependence on fossil fuels.

Even Climate activists are having a difficult time justifying spending millions of dollars more annually for the possibility of reducing our carbon footprint marginally, at best.

Unless you believe that death is imminent, we need to deal with our present inflation problem first before we try and heal our climate issues.

Money always talks and having less of it will be blamed on the present **Administration** come election time.

COMMON SENSE Moment - Climate Change is a Dangerous Game

It is difficult for me to believe that the Climate Change advocates, who are pushing their unrealistic agenda, believe that eliminating fossil fuels here in America will have any significant impact on global emissions or the effect on the ozone layer that they claim will eventually lead to our destruction.

In my opinion, while they may have been able to influence millions of Americans to their cause with claims of apocalyptic disaster, those in charge have another, more sinister reason for creating environmental panic.

The Progressives need to change America from a Capitalist

Society to a Socialist Society and they cannot accomplish that unless they can find an acceptable reason to do so.

They cannot succeed if argued based on the merits alone. Socialism will never be accepted by Americans on face value. We are too bound by our freedoms to ever allow such a change to take place without the help of smoke and mirrors.

In my opinion, Climate Change is being used as a smoke screen that will lead to an anti-growth rather than the pro-growth philosophy we so admire.

In order to diminish Capitalism, you first need to remove the source if its power, which in our case is the energy industry. Just about everything that turns the wheels of prosperity are dependent on energy, specifically fossil fuel energy.

Waiting for renewable energy sources to replace fossil fuels is idealistic at best and an impossible task at worst.

If it is conceivable, we are decades, if not centuries away from developing the scientific expertise to allow wind, solar, plant based or any other source yet to be discovered, to replace the role fossil fuel plays on the global stage.

Even though the Climate Change advocates know all too well that we are years away from producing environmental energy substitutes that can replace them, they are trying to force us into submission immediately, knowing that it will ruin our position on the world stage and destroy Capitalism in the process.

When America achieved energy independence for the first time in half a century, the Progressives saw this as a threat that required immediate action.

Just look at how Russia, one of the other few energy producing nations on the world stage, benefited from our domestic war on energy.

With America producing less gas and oil, the prices began to rise and every other energy producing nation saw their profits begin to soar as the demand rose.

In fact, we now find ourselves needing to rely on others to meet our energy needs once again, a situation that has proven to be costly and problematic over the past decades, when energy was used as a weapon to increase profits for foreign nations or to grant them concessions from America in return for product.

Finally, in my opinion, which is based on the use of my own Common Sense, the Climate Change hierarchy in America, and most likely throughout the globe, are using this cause to start the process of removing Capitalism from its position of importance, which needs to be dismantled BEFORE they can implement the more environmentally friendly system of government called Socialism, or so they claim.

It starts with the loss of energy dominance and ends with a government that uses entitlements and handouts to offset the losses in income and buying power that results when energy costs skyrocket.

Does your Common Sense gene tell you that we are this close to destruction, as the Climate Change activists suggest? Mine does not.

Does your Common Sense gene tell you that America, after destroying our economy and removing our energy dominance, can influence the global environment with our sacrifices while the remaining energy producing countries continue their practices of fossil fuel production as if nothing has changed? Mine does not.

Do the Environmentalists understand that just about EVERYTHING the world manufactures and produces remains dependent on gas, oil or coal to make their products, including plastics, steel, computer chips, electricity and batteries?

(So much for our electric car conversion) I suspect the leaders

understand it but their minions and fervent believers who follow their lead do not.

That's why the Climate Change movement is designed to hinder our economic growth in order to change things.

The threat of environmental ruin is just the means to an end, nothing more. We are in no immediate danger but when time is not on your side, you need to take drastic measures before the public wakes up to your exaggerated claims.

Back to Inflation

Here's the secret that most economist understand but few ideologically based politicians seem to grasp:

- **Heightened Inflation, while impacting all Americans, has a devastating impact on our working class, especially those on the lower economic ladder.**

- **An Inflation Rate of approximately 8% is problematic on its own but it only tells part of the story, especially when those items that you cannot ignore are much higher than the average suggests.**

- **Real life is a lot more complicated than an estimate average rate of Inflation. Gas prices and heating oil are up much higher than the average and that can leave many Americans with no room to manage their budgets. The added cost for them to heat their homes and power their vehicles has risen well above any limited surplus they may have had in the family budget.**

- **It has been said that a large portion of Americans are no more than 2-3 paychecks away from bankruptcy. When the weekly budget can no longer work for your family, it requires drastic action that changes your life in order to make ends meet.**

While the **Progressives a**nd their **Big Tech and Media** partners are trying desperately to convince **Americans** that the fault lies elsewhere, they face a huge uphill battle to change the minds and hearts of **Americans** away from those in power as the source of their problems.

CHAPTER TWELVE

My Own Acknowledged Privilege

I must admit that I do benefit from privilege, though not something that has any racial undertones. My privilege is a result of being raised by parents from the **Greatest Generation**.

They instilled in me a love of God, love of country and an appreciation for being born in **America**. They taught me gratitude for my country rather than finding fault hidden behind every rock.

The pride my parents had in **America** shown brightly and often, leaving a legacy of **Patriotism** instilled in both my brother and I, that shines ever so brilliantly today as it did when we were kids.

Our **Founding Fathers** understood the value of **Patriotism** and its importance for maintaining a vibrant and prosperous America. Here's **Alexander Hamilton**, in his own words on the subject:

"The Safety of a Republic depends essentially on the energy of a common national sentiment; on a uniformity of principles and habits; on the exemptions of the citizens from foreign bias and prejudice; and on a love of country."

Have you noticed that it is not easy to find a **Progressive** that appears to be happy?

Why are they always negative and accusatory about their country? Why is everything always dire and heading for a downfall?

Maybe it has to do their secular approach to life. Christians, as with all religious sects, find solace in knowing that another life for us is on the horizon after this one.

Those that fail to value religion have nothing further to look forward to, which might be a source of their unhappiness.

Whatever the reason, the one thing that all of this unhappiness and disappointment with present day **America** leaves us with is a life that does not value **Patriotism**.

To me, I can think of nothing more disheartening. Love of country and respect for our way of doing things go hand in hand and the need to change everything would leave even the most positive among us in a state of despair.

Finally, I will never apologize for my privilege. In fact, all **Americans** should be grateful they are living in the greatest country on earth.

While we are not perfect nor will we ever be, **America** is the best the planet has to offer and changing it into something else should be fought at every turn and resisted on every level.

Tying Everything Together

As our freedoms slowly begin to erode and we show signs of losing them each day, we can no longer sit on the sidelines.

The best way to do that is to speak up often and with purpose. Silence suggests compliance and that is all the **Progressives** need to continue in their quest to turn **America** into a S**ocialist** nation that no longer represents that shining light on the hill.

Though the rest of the world might be less aware of how the **Progressive Movement** is making inroads in **America**, the entire free world will be feeling the loss if we lose our place as the leader of the free world.

Make no mistake, our position of power on the world stage, because of our freedoms and prosperity, will no longer dominate the global landscape if we allow ourselves to trade freedom and independence for handouts and entitlements.

The Final Word

This is not about politics.

While the **Progressives** may have taken over the **Democratic Party** for the time being, a free and independent **America** cannot sustain itself without a strong and healthy governmental system that prevents either party from going off the rails and risking our independence for ideological reasons.

In other words, a vibrant system of **Checks and Balances,** designed to keep everyone in line, is mandatory, not just a suggestion.

There was a time in our not so distant past where both parties agreed on a number of issues concerning our system of government.

- Both parties shared a concern to defend our nation at all costs and to preserve our freedoms for generations to follow.
- Both parties believed in **Free Speech** and the need to preserve it for the good of the country.
- Both parties agreed that all **Americans**, no matter their race, creed or gender, deserved the same rights and opportunities to succeed without encumbrances that prohibit advancement. In others words, no one should ever be treated differently or receive advantages without having earned them.
- Both parties agreed that we need to protect our borders from both invasion and incursion. In other words, borders have value

> and no one has the right to ignore our laws and enter our country without the proper documentation.

What happened to the era of civil discourse that permitted members of both parties to interact and socialize with members of the opposing party?

What happened to the era when we disagreed on issues but not on the **Constitution?**

When did the opinions of members of the opposing party go from being wrong to being dangerous?

There was a time in our not so distant past where members of both political parties interacted on numerous occasions without any feelings of contempt for the other party, just a belief that they had different opinions of how to proceed with running the government and providing for our citizens.

It's always okay to disagree with your political opponent's views on issues of importance. It's another thing to believe that your opponents represent views that border on evil rather than just a difference of opinion.

In other words, with the rise of power from the **Progressive Movemen**t, we are no longer in an era of disagreement. We have rocketed past civil discourse and headed straight for outright hatred and division.

Any opinion that counters that of the **Progressives**, including moderate views within their own party, need to be silenced and discredited quickly and completely before their blasphemous messages reach the ears of the average **Americans**.

Such an approach to governing can only lead to an atmosphere of conflict between the parties rather than one of civil disagreement.

When you have started the process of radicalizing your followers to the level that permits outright condemnation of different opinions, you have decided that **Free Speech** is a concept that only has merit when the speech in question agrees with yours.

Benjamin Franklin said it best when he proclaimed:

"Without freedom of thought, there can be no such thing as wisdom and no such thing as liberty without freedom of speech."

What makes things more problematic is how our **Media** has decided to take a more active role in promoting the **Progressive** Agenda.

While the **Media** may have exposed their **Bias** long ago, it is much more complicated than that today.

When you hold the nation's communication system in your hands and you decide to go beyond just favoring a position to promoting that position to the masses as if it was undisputed fact, you become a **Protagonist**.

It's the **Protagonists** that become the army for all movements and the **Media** is using their long abandoned shield of neutrality to promote opinion under the guise of objective reporting, hoping that the masses will be fooled into believing these are facts rather than conjecture.

The old adage that **Absolute Power** corrupts **Absolutely** is true. No one should ever be in favor of our government having unlimited power over our citizens.

One of our Founding Fathers, James Madison, said it best many years ago:

"The powers delegated by the Constitution to the Federal Government are few and defined; exercised principally on external objects, as war, peace, negotiation and foreign commerce."

I have always believed that politically, **America** is predominately middle of the road or moderate in philosophy. I still believe that to be true. The extremes of both parties do not represent who the average **American** is or what they believe.

Because the **Progressives** do not represent the average **American**, the **Media** and **Big Tech** understand that they need to convince us that we are still being governed in the middle, which is far from the truth.

Joe Biden was elected in 2020 because we were told that its time to get back to moderation. Joe is a moderate **Democrat** that would bring less chaos and disruption to **America** and re-establish a sense of decorum to the office once again.

If **Joe Biden** was still the man that showed his moderate side decades earlier, there could be some truth to those claims but he is not that man anymore.

Today, **Joe Biden** is a shell of his former self and appears to be guided by the **Progressive** agenda of his handlers rather than his own beliefs.

His obvious frailties and missteps that showcase his decline is the primary reason they keep him away from the press and their unscripted questions, as much as possible. When they can, they use the power of the **Media** to keep many of his missteps and cognitive frailties from ever seeing the light of day.

Every time he addresses the nation for any reason, even minor public appearances, he's reading from a script, which should tell you everything you need to know.

Because of the fact that politics have become so polarized, no one wants to listen to either party when they attempt to convince them that their point of view has merit while their polar opposites offer a less cogent point of view.

The general opinion of the masses is that every politician lies and everyone pretends to care about the people but few do, therefore all of their rants and speeches amount to nothing more than white noise.

Therefore, if we want to alert the masses to the dangers that is represented by the **Progressive** movement, politics is the worst way possible to accomplish that goal.

Sometimes we are better off taking small bites out of their warped ideology by using **Common Sense** logic over political spin.

Luckily for us, much of the **Progressive Agenda** lacks the necessary **Common Sense** logic that would uphold their positions without exposing their radical beliefs.

It is through this lens that we can make the most inroads.

Its time to begin making our voices heard so that we can sway a large number of **Americans** who are not entrenched in any extreme agenda, with **Common Sens**e issues that point out the absurdity of most of the **Progressive** positions.

Let's all be **Common Sense** warriors.

The attack on our Free Speech rights cannot be ignored nor can it be marginalized as something of less importance.

Benjamin Franklin said it best when he helped place it high on the list pf priorities for our new nation:

"Freedom of Speech is a principle pillar of a free government. It is the right of every human being, as far as it does not hurt the right of another; this is the only check it ought to suffer and the only bounds it ought to know."

Politics won't work, the **Media** won't help and **Big Tech** will squelch any attempt to present an alternative view of their agenda.

Common Sense may be our last defense against total **Socialist** control.

I'm asking all **Americans** to make yourselves heard so that the rest of **America** gets to hear both sides, not just the skewed rants of those that pretend to care but prefer we abandon our roots in favor of a kinder and gentler system of government.

One that provides less freedoms and less independence in favor of government dependency and assistance that leaves no room for personal growth or personal accomplishments.

If you think we would be better off being just another country on the global stage, somewhere in the middle of the pack, then you can ignore my advice and deal with whatever is to come.

If you wish to honor our past rather than finding it embarrassing, accept our freedoms rather than apologize for them and cherish our independence rather than find fault with our success, I suggest you take a more active role.

I'll end with a quote from a true patriot that has universal appeal among **Americans** across the country, even though a number of **Progressives** have found him lacking to the point that they would prefer we remove his name from schools and buildings that exalt him as an example of **American** pride:

"I **am a firm believer in the people. If given the truth, they can be depended upon to meet any national crisis. The great point is to bring them the real facts."**

Abraham Lincoln

The End

Printed in the United States
by Baker & Taylor Publisher Services